BUCKSKIN COUNTY WAR

COLORADO TERRITORY SERIES, BOOK I

BUCKSKIN COUNTY WAR

JOHN LEGG

THORNDIKE PRESS
A part of Gale, a Cengage Company

Copyright © 2020 John Legg.
Thorndike Press, a part of Gale, a Cengage Company.

Thorndike Press® Large Print Hardcover Western.
The text of this Large Print edition is unabridged.
Other aspects of the book may vary from the original edition.
Set in 16 pt. Plantin.

LIBRARY OF CONGRESS CIP DATA ON FILE.
CATALOGUING IN PUBLICATION FOR THIS BOOK
IS AVAILABLE FROM THE LIBRARY OF CONGRESS.

ISBN-13: 978-1-4328-9972-1 (hardcover alk. paper)

Published in 2022 by arrangement with Wolfpack Publishing LLC

Printed in Mexico
Print Number : 1   Print Year : 2022

BUCKSKIN COUNTY WAR

CHAPTER 1

Brodie Pike knew he shouldn't get involved. It wasn't any of his business. But after five minutes of watching four gunmen bully some fellow who looked to be a small-time rancher or a farmer, he shook his head and made his decision. He took his hat from where it lay on the table, set it on his head, stood, and moseyed over to the group, then tapped one of the aggressors on the shoulder. When the man turned, Pike pointed at the man being bullied and asked, "Are you afraid of that fella?"

The gunman looked at him as if he were deranged. "What did you say?"

"You heard me."

"What would make you think such a damn fool thing?"

"If you weren't scared of him, it wouldn't take four turnip-headed oafs to harass him."

"Look, pal, this is none of your concern."

"Maybe it ain't. Or wasn't. I'm makin' it

my business."

"What's this man mean to you?"

"Don't know him any more than I know the queen of England. Never saw him before."

"Then what's your interest in him?"

"Just don't like seein' four goat-faced well-heeled pukes trying to intimidate an unarmed man. Now, how's about you let this here fella go on his way, and I'll buy you all a drink."

When the man assessed Pike, he saw a fairly tall man, maybe five-eleven and a hundred seventy pounds. His face had some stubble, but his deep brown eyes were clear and unworried. His green-striped collarless shirt, dark jeans, and boots were of good quality but showed signs of trail wear. His hat was a flat-brimmed, short-crowned Stetson. He wore two Colts in cross-draw holsters. The man did not see the hard look in those brown eyes, and so seemed to take little heed of Pike's dangerousness. "I don't know who the hell you are, mister, but you're startin' to bother me."

"You're about to reduce me to tears."

The man shook his head as if wondering about Pike's sanity. "You know who we are, boy?"

"Nope."

"You know who we work for?"

"Nope."

The man sneered. "We're range detectives workin' for the Buckskin County Cattlemen's Association."

"So?"

The man's voice hardened. "It means, boy, that we are not to be messed with."

"That so?"

"Yep. Now, why don't we buy you a drink, and you can be on your way."

"Reckon not. Not unless this fella leaves with me."

"You keep annoyin' us, the only way you'll be leavin' here is dead." He and his friends laughed.

"I won't be the only one," Pike said flatly.

"You challengin' us?" the first one asked, voice somewhat amused. His companions all turned to face him, spreading out a little.

"Only if you skunks want to die."

There was a frozen moment of silence, then the bartender's voice boomed, "Not in my saloon, boys."

The four gunmen cranked their heads around and looked down the muzzles of two double-barreled shotguns held by the bartender and his assistant.

"You," the barkeep said, "newcomer. Take your new friend and make tracks. The 'detectives' will stay here a spell."

Pike stared at his opponents for a few moments, then looked at the man who had been harried. He jerked his head toward the door. Both headed out.

"Thanks, mister," the man said, relieved.

"Don't need your thanks."

"Sure you do. Those are some bad men. You could've been killed tryin' to help somebody you don't even know."

Pike shrugged, uncomfortable under the praise. "I got two suggestions for you, Mr. . . ."

"Edgar Dunn."

"If I were you, I'd head home right now. And second, I'd avoid this place from now on."

"I was aimin' to head home in the mornin'. Stopped off to have a snort before bunkin' down in the Simpsons' boarding house. And it don't make any difference what saloon a man like me goes in. Those boys'll show up sooner or later."

"A man like you?"

"Small-time rancher. Run a couple dozen head a few miles northwest of here. Several other families too."

"The cattlemen don't like you small-timers gettin' in their way, that it?"

"That's the truth of it. They say we're

10

rustlin' their cattle, so when they decide to raid us, they figured they're justified."

"They haven't yet?"

"Nope. I hear they're waitin' on hirin' more of those gunmen they call detectives. Bunch of gun-totin' sons of bitches. I expect that once enough gun toughs show up, they'll be sendin' assassins after us. They've . . ." He slammed to a stop.

Pike offered a small smile. "Just realized I could be one of them, like those boys who were botherin' you?"

Dunn nodded, suddenly scared.

"Well, I ain't. I'm not a hired gun like those swine, though I reckon I do make my living with these Colts. Well, Mr. Dunn, I wish you well, and I hope you take my advice. Go home and stay home. It's the best way to avoid those vermin."

"Hard to do when we hear they're plannin' to raid our places soon as they get more gun hands."

"Then maybe it's best to stay home and defend your families."

"Reckon a man like you has never been in such a situation." Dunn turned and walked away.

"I'm Marshal Uriah Hanley. Need a word with you, boy," a man of medium height

11

and stocky build said as Pike walked out of his hotel. He held a pistol loosely in his hand and wore a badge on his chest.

"What about?" There was a touch of annoyance in his voice.

"Friend of yours was found dead this mornin'."

"I have no friends here."

"Man you helped last night."

"Never met him before. Don't know who he was. He the one who was killed?"

"Who said anything about him being killed?"

"You said he was dead. If he wasn't killed, you wouldn't be botherin' me on the street while I'm on my way to breakfast."

"You're the obvious suspect."

"Why?"

"You're new in town and were the last man to see Dunn alive."

"No, I wasn't. The last one to see him alive was the man — or men — who killed him. I ain't that man."

"Just come along peaceful, and let's have us a nice chat at my office."

"Reckon not."

The lawman looked a little startled. "I ain't gonna let you just walk away."

"Yes you are."

"You think you can take me?"

12

"Yep."

Hanley smirked. "Even when I got the drop on you?"

Pike feinted with a forearm to the marshal's face but did not hit him. The marshal flinched, and in that second, Pike reached out and snatched the uncocked pistol from the lawman's hand. "Yes," he said quietly. He opened the pistol's loading gate and emptied the shells into his hand, then tossed them into the street. He handed the pistol back to Hanley. "Ain't too many men pulled a gun on me and walked away, Marshal. Consider yourself lucky."

Hanley stood there for a few moments, blinking and trying to take in what had just happened. He found some backbone. "I suggest you get on out of Graystone and stay the hell out. No tellin' what could happen to a stranger who doesn't keep his nose out of places it doesn't belong."

Pike smiled crookedly. "And no tellin' what could happen to a lawman who's in the pocket of the cattlemen. Now, you know damn well who killed Mr. Dunn, and if you want to 'solve' this murder, track them down."

"But . . ."

"Marshal Hanley, I know I didn't do it, and you know I didn't do it. There's no

13

reason for cattlemen to want to get rid of me. I have no reason to go against 'em. I got nothin' against whatever business they're involved in. I took down their boys last night because I hate to see a bunch of pumpkin-headed punks bullying a man who isn't bothering 'em. The cattlemen have nothing to worry about from me."

"How long you plan on stayin' in Gray-stone? Might help if I tell 'em you won't be here more than a day or two."

"I don't really know. Got no place in particular to be. I doubt it'll be very long." It was only a partial lie. He was following some outlaws but didn't know where they were, so he had no certain place to go.

Hanley nodded, knowing he would get no more.

"Where was he found, and what happened to him?"

"Why do you want to know?"

Pike just glared.

"Beaten to death. He was pounded pretty well with fists and boots, I'd say, and maybe with pistols."

"Bad way to die."

"Ain't too many good ones."

"Reckon that's true, but it seems mighty tough for a small-time rancher."

"They're scum. All the ones like him.

14

Damn rustlers and horse thieves, each and every one of 'em. Good riddance to 'em all."

"Mighty amiable way to talk about those folks."

Haney shrugged. "It's better than they really deserve."

Pike ignored that, knowing it would get him nowhere to argue about it. "Where was he found?"

"Road toward his place. Northwest. About a mile out of town."

"How'd you hear about it?" When Haney said nothing, Pike added, "Reckon it was one of the boys who killed him, one of the cattlemen's hired guns. Where's the body?"

"Still there, I reckon. 'Less one of his kind come and got him."

Pike shook his head in disgust. "Did anyone tell the family?"

"Nope. Someone come and told me. I went and took a look."

"And left him there?" Pike asked, incredulous. "You are a real piece of skunk droppin's, Marshal." He stood there glaring at the lawman, fighting with all his might to keep himself from simply shooting the man down. After a few moments, he managed to calm his inner rage. He turned and stalked away.

Haney watched with a combination of

anger and fear as Pike strode off.

Pike breathed deeply and shook his head, which served to calm him a bit more. He was disgusted with himself. If he hadn't helped Dunn, the small-time rancher would've been harassed and maybe roughed up a little, but because Pike had interfered, Dunn had wound up dead. He knew they might've killed Dunn anyway, but that was no balm to his conscience.

He skipped breakfast. Instead, he headed to the livery, where he rented a small wagon and a horse to pull it.

He took the road running northwest out of town. In less than half an hour, he found the body. After climbing down from the wagon, he fired one of his pistols three times to scare off the buzzards that were pecking at it. "Damn birds," he muttered.

He was glad he had had the foresight to bring a blanket. He used it to wrap the body and set it in the bed of the wagon, then reloaded his Colt, climbed onto the wagon seat, and slowly moved down the road. About an hour later, he topped a very low rise and spotted a large simple cabin made of logs taken from the pine-covered mountainside not far to the northwest. It had a window on each side of the door and a portico across the whole front. A similarly constructed barn was behind and to the left of the house, as was a chicken coop. A vegetable garden stretched out from the right side of the house and looked to be flourishing. A corral, holding perhaps a dozen horses and mules, was to the left.

CHAPTER 2

Pike slowed when he saw two men trotting across the broad meadow toward him. The two stopped and bent toward each other, then one nodded and peeled off, galloping to the north. Pike shoved his jacket aside, clearing the path to his Colts.

He stopped the wagon as the man pulled up alongside the cart's horse. The man was in his early twenties. He wore a time-worn wide-brimmed hat with a deep, dark sweat stain around the bottom of the crown, a plain gray cotton shirt with a pocket that appeared to hold cigarette fixings, sturdy denim pants, and manure- and mud-covered boots. His face, hands, and posture indicated he was a hard man — not in Pike's way, but one inured to hard labor and adversity.

"What's your business here, mister?" he asked.

Pike just stared at him.

"I asked you what your business is here."

More silence from Pike.

"Dammit, man, answer me!"

"And good day to you, too," Pike said, sarcasm dripping from his voice.

Anger crossed the man's face. "I don't cotton to folks like you."

"Folks like me?"

"You got the look of a gunman about you, and the only one with hired guns around these parts is Ulysses Hungerford."

"Don't know him any more than I do you." Pike noticed that a flicker of doubt crossed the man's face. "And I don't hire my gun out." It was said with some heat.

They stared at each other for some moments before the cowboy asked, "What's in the wagon?"

"You know, mister, you might get answers if you were to use some manners and ask politely."

"This is my land, and I'll ask whatever the hell I want however I want."

"Then you'll be short on answers, 'least from this fella." More glaring, then Pike relented in a manner of speaking by asking, "You know a fella named Edgar Dunn?"

"My brother," the man responded warily. "Why?"

"Body's in the back."

19

The cowpoke moved forward, then leaned over in the saddle, and pulled the blanket away from the man's corpse a little. "What the hell'd you do to him?" he asked, voice a mixture of anger and grief.

"Nothing but bring him back here so kin can give him a decent burial."

"Like hell! You . . ." He stopped as the man who had ridden off earlier galloped up with two companions; they formed a semi-circle in front of Pike. The three were built and dressed much like the first: medium size, work- and sun-worn faces, drab, well-worn clothes and boots, and six-guns worn uncomfortably around their waists.

The former saw the first one's face and asked, "What's goin' on, Clay?"

"Ed's been killed. This son of a bitch has Ed's body in the wagon here. Stomped him to death."

The three, joined by Clay, started to unlimber their Colts.

"Don't do it, boys. It's bad enough one of your family is dead. No need to add to the count."

"You think you can take all four of us?" one of the newcomers asked. He looked scared but determined.

"Yes." It was a simple statement

Time froze, then the second newcomer

asked somewhat uncertainly, "You mind takin' off your hat, mister?"

Pike stared at him for a second or two, then shrugged and did as he was asked.

The newcomer nodded. "This man didn't kill Ed."

"How do you know that?" Clay asked.

"Hubert saw him help Ed at the Buckskin Saloon last night. Hubert left town just after that, but Edgar spent the night there. He described Ed's helper to me. Made him take off his hat just now so I could see his face. I'm sure this is the man who helped Ed."

"Helped him how?"

"Four of those scum hired by Hungerford was roughin' Ed up, and this man stepped in and stopped it. Looked ready to shoot it out with the four. Bartenders pulled out their scatterguns and told Ed and this fella to hightail it. Kept the four swine there for a spell." He rode forward until he was alongside Pike. "Name's Charlie McAllister, Edgar's brother-in-law. He's married — was married — to my sister. Nice to meet ya, though I wish it were under better circumstances."

Pike nodded and shook the man's hand. "Name's Brodie Pike."

"These others are Clay Dunn, Edgar's brother; Connor Felder, a cousin; and Matt

21

McAllister, my oldest son."

"So, what happened?" Dunn asked.

"Not now, Clay," Charlie said. "Let's get Ed home and then talk. Matt, hurry on to the house and tell the family what's gone on, then head to Ed's and get Cora."

The younger man turned his horse and loped off.

"Follow us, Mr. Pike, if you please. This place is mine. Edgar's is a mile or so west, but we'll take care of him here."

A few minutes later, Pike stopped about ten yards from the house at Charlie's command. Two boys in their early teens came out of the house.

"They'll take care of Ed now, Mr. Pike." As the two carefully carried Dunn's body into the house, Charlie nodded. "Please drive the wagon into the barn, Mr. Pike. Someone'll take care of the horse."

After he had done so, McCallister, Dunn, and Felder escorted Pike into the house. He almost smiled at the wariness they accorded him, but he was impressed, too. They knew him to be a gunman, but they were determined to keep a close eye on him, though wary enough to not give him much maneuvering room.

The inside of the house was better appointed than Pike had assumed. The furniture was crafted by hand but well-made and cared for, including a long table with six chairs. Two thickly upholstered chairs sat in corners. A rocking chair and a spinning wheel were next to the fireplace. To the left was the kitchen, with a large cast-iron stove, a rudimentary set of shelves holding various foodstuffs, and a finely crafted cabinet with dishes. A coffeepot and a stewpot sat on the stove. Two rooms led off from the rear of the area.

"Sit, Mr. Pike," Charlie said as he and the other men removed their hats and hung them on pegs on the wall near the door. A young woman came out of a back room. "Some food and coffee for our guest, Marcy." He looked at Pike. "Something a little stronger with your food?"

"Nope." A moment later, the young woman set a bowl of thick, savory-smelling stew and a mug of coffee in front of Pike. Having not had breakfast, Pike was hungry, and he dug in.

The Dunn and McAllister men took seats, and Clay Dunn said, "So tell us what happened." His tone was no more polite than it had been.

Between mouthfuls of stew and coffee, Pike said, "Right after we left the saloon, I bid Mr. Dunn goodbye. Never saw him again. This mornin', the marshal confronted me and told me Mr. Dunn's body had been found. He hinted that I was responsible. I disabused him of that notion. He told me where Mr. Dunn's body was found. Said he left it there."

"Son of a bitch!" McAllister snapped.

Pike nodded. "I rented the wagon and horse, got Mr. Dunn's body, and headed here."

The silence grew, and Pike finished his meal.

Finally, Felder asked, "Do you plan to do anything about this?"

"Nope. Ain't my problem."

"What the hell do you mean, boy?" Dunn demanded. "It weren't for you, Ed'd still be alive."

Pike knew that, and it bothered him. He knew he should not have interfered, but there was little he could do about it. "Just what do you think I should do?" he asked, not quite sarcastically.

"Find the bastards who killed Ed and kill 'em."

"Just like that, eh?" The sarcasm was undisguised this time.

"You're a gunman, and by your attitude, you must think you're a good one. It shouldn't be hard for you to do."

24

"Maybe. But who did it?"

"Must've been the ones who was givin' Ed a hard time at the saloon."

"Could be. Could be any of that fella Hungerford's men, however many of those hard cases he hired."

"They're the only ones. Don't matter anyway," Dunn snapped. "Killin' any of 'em would be good."

"Reckon it would. Be mighty foolish, though."

"Just like I thought. You're a lily-livered son of a bitch."

Pike glared at him, then turned his gaze on Charlie McAllister. "Was he born this stupid, or did one of you teach him?"

"Why you bastard," Dunn snapped, shoving himself up angrily.

"Sit down and shut up, Clay," McAllister said in a tight voice. "Would it help if we paid you, Mr. Pike? We ain't got much, but we could come up with some cash."

Pike shook his head. "Money don't enter into it. It's just foolish."

The men paused when Matt McAllister came in, followed by a woman Pike figured was Cora Dunn. She was pale-faced and went straight to one of the rear bedrooms. Moments later, crying could be heard from the room.

Dunn, who had sat back down, looked ready to stand again and send another epithet Pike's way but did not do either when McAllister shot him an angry glace.

"Why would it be foolish?" McAllister asked.

"I'd like to know, too," Connor Felder added.

"Put you and your families in more danger than they already are," Pike said flatly.

"How can that be?" Felder asked. "There'd be four less of those gun-totin' bastards around."

"I maybe could kill one of them or four, or even ten of those boys, though I don't think there's that many, judgin' by what Mr. Dunn told me last night and what I just heard here. Anyway, if I kill one or a dozen, it won't make much of a difference. Ed said Hungerford's waitin' for more shooters. If I kill some, he'll just hire more. It might take a bit for the new ones to arrive, but when Hungerford decides to move against you, it'll be even harder on you than it might be otherwise. I get the idea that Hungerford hasn't harassed you much so far."

"Not yet," McAllister said. "Like you said, we think he's waitin' to hire more gunmen, though with the ones he's got now, he could cause us a heap of trouble."

Pike nodded.

"Why would Hungerford suddenly increase his persecution of us?" Felder asked, somewhat perplexed. "Wouldn't he send his men after you?"

"Likely he would."

"Then why would he come against us?"

"Because," McAllister said, suddenly understanding, "Hungerford'll figure we hired him, or even just that he was somehow allied with us. Ain't that right, Mr. Pike?"

"It is."

"But won't he come against us harder after they killed Ed so easily and boldly?" Felder asked.

"They might, but I doubt it. They'll figure this was a strong warnin' to you folks, especially since they just left him out there to be found by anybody travelin' that road. And for the buzzards to feast on."

Rage splashed across all the men's faces. "Them cold-blooded devils!" McAllister spat.

CHAPTER 3

It took a bit for McAllister to calm down enough to speak again. "So, what do you suggest we do, Mr. Pike?"

"Can't tell you that. It's all up to you."

"You sure you won't hire on with us?"

"I'm sure."

McAllister stood there thinking, then asked, "Do you have any suggestions on what we can do?"

Pike sighed. Once again, he regretted having gotten involved. Worse, his better nature wanted to help these people, but his common sense told him he would be wise to stay out of it. There was, he figured, no good end to come from all this. It had already become a mess like it too often did when he tried to do the right thing. His staying here, he figured, would only make it worse.

"Your choices are mighty limited," he said.

"But we do have choices?" Felder asked.

"None that you'll like," he said.

"Let's hear 'em anyway," McAllister said. His voice was still angry, but there was a note of fear, or maybe despair, in it too.

"First off, you could go after them." He ignored the gasps. "You ain't gunmen, but you could bushwhack 'em. Or burn 'em out."

"But after the first one or two, they'd come down on us like hellfire, wouldn't they?" Felder asked.

"For certain they would." McAllister shook off a shudder.

"Other options?"

"Keep an eye on 'em. If it looks like they're about to come raise hell here, fort up, either here or at one of your other places that might be more fortified. Keep yourselves close to home. Have a couple boys go out every day to care for the cattle and take care of whatever else needs doin'."

"That'd be even more foolish," Felder interjected. "They'd just pick off whoever was tendin' cows, or burn down the other houses and run off that stock."

"You're learnin', Mr. Felder."

"Any other suggestions?" Dunn asked, his sarcasm overriding his sense and fear.

"Leave." It was said flatly and harshly.

"Leave?" Clay exploded. He was so angry he simply sputtered, unable to get another word out.

"This is our land, Mr. Pike," McAllister said more calmly. "Our livelihood. We worked hard to get this land and to improve it. We worked hard to better ourselves."

"And you've done well, far's I can see. But there's somethin' else you need to consider."

"What's that?"

"Your families. You have to decide if the risk to your wives and young'uns is worth the price of this land and the cattle. I don't know this Hungerford, but I've known others like him. He won't give up 'til he has this land and has killed you all or driven you out."

"You're right, Mr. Pike, I don't like any of them options. I don't cotton to runnin', though."

"Most good men don't, Mr. McAllister."

"Don't seem to bother you none," Clay snapped.

Pike shot him a cold look, but McAllister said, "Shut up, Clay. I figure this man won't run from anything that needs handlin', but like he said, this ain't his fight." He looked at Pike. "So, you suggest we just up and leave?"

"I ain't suggestin' anything, just givin' you what options you have as I see 'em. But there might be an option that can get you out of here safely without runnin'."

"What's that?" McAllister tried to fight back a sudden spark of hope.

"Sell out to Hungerford."

"What?" Clay exploded again. "Why, that's . . ."

"Shut up, Clay. Dammit, I'm tired of you makin' an ass of yourself. Mr. Pike here's gonna think we're all a bunch of damn fools because of you. I don't want to hear another peep out of you." He paused for a moment, then said, "Sorry, Mr. Pike."

"No need to apologize, Mr. McAllister. Every family's got at least one idiot."

A very small smiled touched McAllister's lips, then vanished in an instant. "Do you think that'd work?"

"Hell, I don't know. He might not make a deal since he thinks he can run you off and it won't cost anything. On the other hand, he might figure it's easier to buy you out and not have to pay a bunch of mercenaries."

"Why ain't he just sent over the lackeys he's already hired all at once and burned our homes and killed us when we ran?" Felder asked, suppressing a shiver.

"If he's the kind of man I'm thinkin' he is, he's evil, but he's not a fool. He might have the local law, maybe even the governor in his pocket, but if he went and killed a couple dozen men, women, and children, it might not sit well with the governor or a senator who might be lookin' for re-election. And it might bring federal marshals, or even the Army, down on him."

"That makes sense, I reckon."

"When I was in the saloon and braced those four boys, they said something about being range detectives workin' for the Buckskin County Cattlemen's Association."

"Detectives. That's a hoot," Felder said with a shake of his head.

"I assume there's more men involved than just Hungerford."

Both Felder and McAllister nodded. "Miles Appleyard," the latter said, "Harland Barrington, Reuben Darrow, and Granville Forsythe."

"Might be them keepin' Hungerford in line somewhat, too. They might have enough sense to know what a full-out assault on you folks would mean, even if he doesn't."

"I still don't like 'em."

"Ain't sayin' you should. I reckon they're as bad as he is, but maybe a bit more cautious. It might mean that if I went after their gunmen, they'd lose their caution and allow their 'detectives' to come full-out against you."

McAllister and the others cast worried glances at each other.

"I don't know if that's true, of course, but if it is, you might have a better chance of negotiatin'. If they ain't as hell-bent on killin' folks as you think Hungerford is, they might be willin' to talk."

McAllister and the others thought that over and finally nodded at each other. "Any idea how we might go about it without gettin' ourselves killed?"

"Might be hard — hell, might not be possible — but try to find yourselves someone you can trust even somewhat in town. A lawyer, maybe. Someone who ain't in the association's employ. Have him make arrangements for a sit-down with Hungerford, or better yet, some of the others if you think they might be more reasonable."

"We ain't likely to find someone like that," Felder said, his smidgen of hope fading.

"Then write a letter to one of 'em. Have one of Hungerford's town minions take it to him. The marshal might be the one, or some judge. Or hell, one of you ride out there some night and slip it under his door. Then you wait to see if they're willin' to talk."

"Then what?"

"If he is, meet him or them and make an offer."

"Just for the land? What about the cattle and houses and all?"

"Take that into account. Do you want to sell him all the cattle? Keep some for yourselves to start elsewhere? Figure in the water rights and improvements, then make your offer. He might do so first, but I reckon he'll likely let you have the first move. Make your offer a little high, but not too much. You ask too much, he'll flat out say no, but you need some room to negotiate — if he's willing. He might not be. He might just offer you some insultin' price and tell you to take it or leave it."

"What then?" Felder asked.

"Then we're right back where we are now," McAllister said. "No better, no worse."

"Can't be sure of that neither," Pike said. "He and the others might figure that if you were willin' to sell, you just might take their offensive offer if they put more pressure on you."

"Which they'll likely do sooner or later anyway," McAllister interjected, "leavin' us right where we are."

"Afraid so."

"What do you think is best?" Felder asked, all hope gone.

"You folks have to decide that for yourselves."

"Any thoughts on which you think is best?"

"Depends on the swine runnin' the association. From what I've heard from you and the little I've seen, Hungerford is scum. I know nothin' about the others, but if there's one or two who seem a little less onerous, offerin' to sell might be the best. 'Course, they might be as bad a Hungerford, or worse. If none of 'em seems even partly decent, pullin' up stakes and movin' out would be the best, I'd say."

McAllister drew in a long breath and let it out slowly. "We don't have much of a future, do we?" he said glumly.

"Not here, you don't."

There was a long silence before McAllister said, "Well, you gave us a heap to think about, Mr. Pike. We're obliged for what you did for Ed. You're welcome to stay the night, though you'll have to sleep in the barn."

"Reckon I'll head back to town. Got to get the wagon back. I'll stay the night there, then pull out in the mornin'."

McAllister nodded at a boy about ten or eleven years old, who headed out.

"Where to?" Felder asked.

"Ain't sure, but likely Sharpsville. I been trackin' a few boys, and I hear they might be enjoyin' their ill-gotten gains there."

Dunn snorted. "So, you'll go chasin' fellas for the bounty, but you won't help some honest folks facin' men that're as bad, maybe worse? And got bounties on 'em, too, I reckon, that you could collect?"

Before Pike could respond, McAllister backhanded him across the face, knocking Dunn out of the chair. "You insult our guest one more time, Clay, and I'll kill you if he don't." He turned. "Sorry, Mr. Pike."

"Like I said, there's at least one idiot in every family."

McAllister grunted an affirmative. "Well, if you're gonna head back to town, you best do so. You'll be lucky to make it before dark. Me and my kin here have a lot to discuss after takin' care of Ed. My son Abe will have cared for the horse."

Pike shook hands with all of them but Clay Dunn. "I hope you can find a solution that'll cause the least damage to your families."

In the barn, it was but a few minutes before the youth finished hitching up the small wagon. The horse had been fed and watered. Pike climbed onto the wagon seat and tossed the boy a fifty-cent piece. "Don't tell your folks," he said with a small grin.

"I won't," the boy said, staring at the coin as if he had just been handed a king's ransom.

Pike clucked to the horse and got moving. As he drove across the valley, he again cursed himself for having gotten involved even as little as he had. He also cursed himself as being responsible for Edgar Dunn's death. For a few moments, he considered turning around and offering to help these folks, but he fought off the thought. It would, he figured, only cause them more trouble, and it would likely turn out bad, like that time he had taken on the job of finding a woman at her father's request . . .

Chapter 4

It was almost four years ago when he had been hired to find Dinah Wilkins. That had been farther north in Colorado Territory. Asa Wilkins said Dinah had been abducted by an outlaw named Micah Bruckner. Wilkins assumed his daughter would be ravished and possibly killed, so he wanted her found before any harm or abuse could come to her.

"How long's she been gone?" Pike asked.

"Three days."

"Three days?" Pike said, dumbfounded. "Unless they've been on the run ever since without stopping, she was violated long ago."

"I can't believe that," Wilkins insisted.

"Think what you like, Mr. Wilkins, but I've been dealing with such men for a long time, and they don't hesitate to abuse women any chance they get. These are not upstanding citizens we're talking about."

"Just get her back." He handed Pike a wanted poster. "And soon. I'll pay you five hundred dollars."

"That's a heap of money."

"Not to me, and not for my daughter's return."

"Which way did they go, do you know?"

"I think northeast, toward Denver."

Pike shrugged, put on his hat, and left. Even with all the time that had passed — three days in Pike's business was a long time to capture outlaws — Pike didn't have much trouble picking up the abductors' trail.

But it took two days of hard riding before he closed in on them. It was edging toward late afternoon when he saw smoke drifting up from a small stand of cottonwoods and willows along a wide, shallow stream he had been following. He stopped about a quarter-mile away and loosened the horse's saddle and allowed it to drink. Pike knelt and drank also, then washed his hands and face, scrubbing off the dust and sweat of the tough ride.

Figuring there was no reason to wait, he cinched up the saddle, mounted, and rode forward. At the edge of the trees, he dismounted and tied off his horse. He checked his revolvers, then started moving through the copse. He slowed when he heard voices, then crept forward until he was hidden by the drooping boughs of a weeping willow and surveyed the camp.

He spotted the young woman resting against a tree, head lolling a little as she sat quietly. He was surprised to see that she seemed to be in no peril. She was not tied up, her clothing was not disheveled except by the rumpling brought on by travel, and she appeared to be relaxed.

There were two men in camp, neither looking like hardened outlaws, though they were armed. One was caring for the horses, and the other was butchering a small deer that was hanging from a low cottonwood branch.

Pike eased out a pistol, then said loudly, "Micah Bruckner, you and your pal throw down your weapons and lay flat on the ground."

"Who are you, and what do you want?" the one butchering the deer said, not moving. His voice quavered.

"Take the woman back home and turn you into the law back in Westerville."

"What for?"

"Robbing a bank, killin' some folks, and stealin' Miz Wilkins."

"I didn't do none of that. I never killed nobody, and me and Dinah are elopin'."

" 'Fraid I don't believe you."

"You gotta, mister. I ain't no bad man." The quake in his voice had grown.

A twig snapped behind Pike, and without hesitation, he shot Bruckner in the back. Someone clubbed Pike in the back of the head, and he sank to his knees, then fell sideways, causing whoever it was behind him to miss with a second swing with the small log. He landed on his shoulder and half-rolled. From his back, he fired twice at his assailant. One slug thudded into the log, knocking it loose, and the other hit the man in the sternum, driving slivers of bone into his heart and lungs.

Pike rose and looked into the clearing. The woman was hovering over Bruckner and sobbing heavily. The third man was hurriedly saddling a horse. He walked toward Bruckner, reloading his Colt as he did.

The woman looked at him with tears of sorrow and anger in her eyes. "You no-good . . ."

"Hush, Miss."

She stayed where she was, the tears continuing to flow.

Pike looked down at the man, who was still alive but probably wouldn't be for long. "Should've given up straight off, friend. I would've just taken Miz Wilkins home and

41

you to the nearest town to collect my bounty."

"Didn't do anything wrong," the man offered, his words coming laboriously.

Pike pulled a paper from his shirt pocket and held it out before Bruckner's eyes, "This is you, ain't it?"

"That's my name and likeness, but the rest of it ain't true. I did rob a bank a while back, but anything wrong I did was all in the past. I been straight for a year now, ever since I met Dinah."

Pike didn't believe him and said so.

Bruckner was quiet for a few moments, then said, "I told you, I didn't kidnap her. We were goin' to Denver to get married."

"Bad timin' and bad luck for you when you stole off with her."

"Dammit, I didn't."

"He's tellin' the truth," Dinah said through her sobs.

"Still don't believe him. Or you." But he was beginning to have some doubt.

"You just gonna leave me here?" Bruckner asked, voice weak and full of pain.

"Nothin' I can do for you."

" 'Cept put me out of misery."

"That what you want?"

"Reckon I'm done for anyway. Might's well make it fast 'stead of leavin' me here

42

bleedin' to death."

Pike nodded once sharply. "Dinah, go on over behind those trees where you were before."

"No, I'm stayin' here with Micah."

"This won't be pretty, ma'am. It'd be best you go over there and then come back to cry over him when it's over and done."

She did as she was told. Without emotion, Pike fired a bullet into Bruckner's heart. He turned as Dinah rushed past him to wail over her dead lover's body.

Pike heard a horse being ridden away fast. He didn't much care. The young woman was free, and he could bring her home. He didn't need to go chasing another outlaw for the hell of it, or even for a reward if there were one on his head. He touched the woman, who was still moaning her loss over Bruckner, lightly on the shoulder. "Miz Wilkins?" he said. "I've come to take you home. Your pa's some worried about you."

"Go to blazes, mister," Dinah said, shocking Pike. "You killed him! Shot him in the back!"

"But these outlaws stole you away from your home. Why are you grievin' for one of 'em?"

"What do you know, you insufferable idiot?" she said, swinging her tear-stained

43

face around to look at him. "He's not an outlaw, and he didn't kidnap me. I went willingly with Micah because I loved him, and he loved me. We were going to go to Denver and get married there. We both told you that. Why don't you believe us?"

Once again, Pike was shocked. "You were gonna marry an outlaw?"

"He's no outlaw. No longer anyway, like he told you. He's a decent man and was going to take me away from that repulsive old goat who calls himself my father."

"Asa's not your father?"

"He is by blood but as far as I'm concerned, not by feelings or decency."

"You've seen the paper showin' there's a reward on Micah. That makes him an outlaw."

"That's from someone who's a liar, who accused him of something he didn't do."

"He didn't kill three people and rob the bank in Westerville?"

"He didn't do any of that," she insisted.

Pike shook his head in disbelief. "Well, what am I gonna do with you now? If your father is abusive, as you indicate he is, and your outlaw lover is dead, your choices are limited."

"Take me with you."

"Nope. I don't rightly know where I'm

going, and no idea what I'm gonna do when I get there. And I don't need to be totin' some addle-pated woman with me."

"Not very chivalrous of you."

"I can be chivalrous when called for. This just happens to not be one of those times."

"Then what am I gonna do?" she wailed.

"I'll take you as far as Westerville. Bruckner has a reward on him, like I said, and I aim to claim it. I expect there's one on his dead pal, too. Once we get there, you'll be on your own."

She started to cry again. "That won't help much," she howled. "Only choice for a girl like me is in a parlor house, or so I've heard. There's no other jobs for women."

Pike sucked in a breath, then let it out slowly. "You know how to butcher a deer?" he suddenly asked.

"I think so." She looked at him with a question in her eye.

"Start doin' so. Just enough meat for the two of us. It'll be dark shortly, and I'm hungry."

"Why don't you do it?"

"I have other work to do."

"Like what?"

"Tending to things."

"What?" Her mouth widened into an O, and she glanced down at Bruckner's body.

45

"Oh," she added glumly, tears flowing again. But she got up, found the knife Bruckner had been using, picked it up, and wiped it off on her dress. Then she stood there, tears streaming down her face.

Pike was tempted to just drag the body out of the way, but he decided that would be a horrible thing to do in front of Dinah, even if Bruckner was an outlaw. She wasn't, and she didn't deserve to be subjected to such a spectacle. Instead, he bent and lifted the man and walked off a ways into the trees, where he found three horses. He dropped the body and began to saddle the horses.

Before long, Dinah shouted listlessly, "Food's almost ready."

"Be there directly." He tossed Bruckner's body over one saddle and tied it down. In the new darkness, he walked across the little camp to get his own horse, unsaddle it, and tend it. He hobbled the mount and turned it out to graze and drink. He let the other body lay where it was. He would take care of it later. Finally, he went over and flopped down by the fire.

Dinah handed him a tin plate with a slab of venison and set a tin cup of coffee beside him. "Thanks," he said, pulling out his knife. He cut off a piece and stuck it in his

46

mouth, chewing slowly. "What's the other dead fellow's name? The dead one who beaned me?"

"Micah just called him Chas."

"And the one who run off?"

"Chub Pickett."

"Hell of a name."

Dinah shrugged and picked at her food, eyes swollen and red.

After eating, Pike went and got Chas's body and tied it over another horse. Done, he went back to the fire and poured himself another cup of coffee. He drank it slowly but finished soon enough. "Best get some sleep, Miz Wilkins. We got a long ride tomorrow."

"Don't know if I can sleep with Micah . . ." she said, beginning to cry again.

"Do your best." Without another thought, Pike took to his bedroll and struggled to sleep because of the throbbing in his skull from being hit, the ache in his injured shoulder, and a growing sense of doubt about Bruckner's outlaw status.

CHAPTER 6

They left just after dawn, Pike leading the way, towing the horses holding the bodies. Dinah brought up the rear. That concerned Pike a bit; he wondered if she had a gun hidden somewhere in her voluminous dress. An hour or so later, she pulled up next to him.

"Mind if I ride alongside you?" she asked quietly.

"Nope. Be a pleasure to have such pretty company. But I'm mighty surprised considerin' what you must think of me."

"It's better than ridin' at the back lookin' at . . . lookin' at . . ." she said with a small, bitter smile on her full pink lips.

He nodded.

"How long have you been killing men for a living?"

Pike bit back the retort that had quickly formed. In a reasonable tone, he countered, "How long you been sleepin' with outlaws?"

Dinah looked as if she had been slapped in the face. "How dare you say such a thing! You're even more horrible than I first thought."

"Askin' me about bein' a man-killer is a ladylike question?"

She thought for a moment. "I suppose not. Guess I asked for your response."

"That you did, ma'am."

She was silent, then said, "Maybe I asked wrong. What I'd like to know is how long you've been a manhunter?"

"Too long, I sometimes think. Roundin' up miscreants ain't a fun chore, nor easy. Comes with a heap of risk sometimes."

"And rewards, too."

"Yep. I sometimes wonder, though, if the rewards are enough for me to take the risks."

"Why'd you start doing it, then?"

He shrugged. "Didn't have much choice, I reckon. When I come out of the war, jobs were mighty scarce. Some ex-soldiers . . ."

"Which side?"

"Doesn't matter. They raided a farmhouse, claimin' to be lookin' for food. They killed the farmer, his wife, and four young'uns." He ignored Dinah's gasp of shock. "County sheriff asked me to join the posse since I knew how to handle a gun. Took a while, but we caught up with 'em, and justice was served." His face was tight.

"You're bothered by that, aren't you? You — or the others — killed them, and that bothers you."

"It's never pleasant killin' someone, even if he is a devil in man's clothing. Often necessary with such demons, but never pleasant."

"Apparently you're pretty good at it, though." She could not keep the animosity out of her voice.

"Yep. Years of bein' in positions where it was necessary."

"A matter of them or you?"

"Yes'm."

"You ever think of doing something else? Something less dangerous and damaging of the spirit?"

Pike thought she sounded a little less hostile. "I've considered it from time to time," Pike said with a note of wistfulness in his voice. "Don't know what else I'd do, though. I ain't cut out to be a farmer, and I have no skills in any trade. I suppose I could try my hand at ranchin' or raisin' horses, but that doesn't appeal to me much either."

"Didn't you learn anything but shooting in the Army?"

Pike grinned ruefully. "No, ma'am, not really. I was a sniper."

"Oh! That's not a very good civilian trade."

"Not usually, no." He paused, then asked, "What about you? How'd a pretty, well-off girl like you get caught up with a man like Micah Bruckner?"

The antagonism returned. "Micah worked for Pa for a spell, and I got to know him. Then I fell in love with him, and he returned those feelings. He went to Pa and asked if he could marry me. Pa told him he was no good and not worthy of me."

"I'd have to say he was probably right about that."

"Pshaw. It might be true, but I doubt it. Pa just wanted to keep me to himself."

"He seemed mighty eager to get you back."

"Reckon he was, but only so I couldn't tell folks what kind of man he really is."

Pike said nothing. He was thinking she had turned at least a little of her enmity from him onto her father.

"Micah left in a huff after Pa warned him not to come near me again," she continued. "We met a few times after that. Micah told me he was gonna go off and make some money, then he was gonna come back and get me and we'd ride off to somewhere, maybe Denver, to tie the knot."

"That when he got into trouble?"

Dinah nodded sadly. "I knew he had robbed one bank, maybe two, but he never killed anyone. He was a good man, but he went bad because of me." She fought back tears.

"Ain't your fault, Miz Dinah," he said, knowing the feeling. "He could've come up with money in legal ways. Even if he robbed a bank, he didn't have to kill anyone. That was all his doin'. It had nothin' to do with you."

"You're very kind to say that. But he didn't kill anyone," she insisted. "And even if it was true, nothing can be done about any of it now. I just have to live with what happened and try to figure out what to do with my life."

"We'll figure something out."

"We?"

"I can't let you just mosey on off to a cathouse 'cause there's nothing else to do. Not since I left you grievin', even if it was necessary."

"You're crazy," she snapped.

Pike gave it considerable thought as they rode but had come to no conclusion when they arrived in Westerville late in the afternoon. As they moved slowly down the main street, a medium-height, thickset man of about forty moved in front of them. Pike and Dinah stopped.

"I'm Marshal Jud Collier. Whatcha got here?"

"Couple boys who robbed the bank and killed three people a while back."

Collier's eyes widened, and he moved around to lift each man's head. "Don't know these boys for sure, but I think they did rob the bank here. That was about a year ago, though. They didn't get much, and there was only a hundred-dollar reward for the two of them. Posse gave chase for a little, then let it drop. Weren't worth the effort."

Dinah looked at Pike with a look of triumph. "Told you," she said angrily.

Collier suddenly rested his hand on his pistol grip. "Why'd you go and shoot these boys? One of 'em in the back? A small-time bank robbery doesn't deserve a death sentence."

Pike stiffened. He reached into his shirt pocket, pulled out the wanted poster, and handed it to Collier.

The marshal looked it over. "That ain't from anyone here. Don't have it from anywhere else, and when he did rob the bank here, they didn't kill anyone. You're either a liar or you've been deceived, mister."

"Hell and damnation!" Pike hissed.

"What's your name?" Collier asked.

"Brodie Pike."

"I've heard of you. Wouldn't expect an experienced bounty hunter like you to be hoodwinked."

Pike clamped his mouth shut, teeth gritted, trying to hold back the anger that had erupted within him.

"Who is the young lady? And what was she doin' with these boys?"

"Her pa said she was kidnapped by them," Pike said hastily before Dinah could say anything. "Over near Arvada. I was in town when it happened. Her pa heard and asked me to find her."

Collier nodded. "I expect you're aimin' to get the reward, small as it might be?"

"No," Pike said, feeling sick with humiliation at having been duped.

"All right, take the bodies down to the undertakers — three blocks down and then left on Buffalo Street," Collier said tightly.

Pike nodded with a sigh. "A good hotel and restaurant?"

"The Regent," Collier said, pointing at a building a few doors down on the other side of the street, "has both. A mite pricey, though. Two blocks down on this side is the Capital. A bit cheaper, but still fairly good." He looked at Dinah. "Can I help you in any way, ma'am?"

Dinah thought it over for a minute, then shook her head. Though she disliked Pike and hated him even, she at least knew him, and she sensed he was remorseful for what he had done. She didn't know the lawman.

Pike, Dinah, and their grisly cargo headed down the street. Less than an hour later, the bodies had been delivered, the horses were in the livery, Pike and Dinah each had a room at the Capital, and they were sitting down to a meal at the hotel's restaurant.

As they ate — pork chops, potatoes and corn for him, chicken and dumplings for her — Pike hesitatingly asked, "Do you have kinfolk or friends anywhere who could take you in?"

Dinah thought for a bit, then said, "I have a cousin in Boulder."

"He someone who can be trusted?"

"She. Her name's Lacy, and I think she can. Why?"

"Maybe you can go there to live. At least 'til you get on your feet and can figure out what to do as time passes. But you must be sure you can trust her."

"I'm certain I can. We practically grew up

together 'til she got married and moved to Denver. They moved on to Boulder year before last."

"That's maybe a new problem, trustin' her husband. Can you?"

"I think so, but I ain't sure." She grimaced. "I'd like to think Lacy made a better choice in a man than I did."

"Sometimes folks fall in love with the wrong people. You ain't the only one who's done so." He paused. "Though considerin' what's happened, maybe it wasn't all that bad a choice." He frowned.

"You ever done so?"

"No, not really. But she did."

"What's that mean?"

"Means she fell in love with me, and I was the wrong man for her. And it cost her everything."

"What did it cost?"

"Her life."

Even though she knew that Pike was a hard man in a hard job and her anger at him had lessened only a little, she was shocked. "What happened?" she finally asked in a soft, worried voice.

"That is something you don't need to know and have no business knowin'."

"Were you gonna marry her?"

"I was thinking seriously about doin' so."

56

"And I bet you ain't thought of doing so ever since. Am I right?"

"Yep, you are. No woman with any sense'd marry me, and I ain't foolish enough to ask."

"Because you're a bounty hunter?"

"Yep. Dangerous enough for me, more so for a woman."

"Don't you ever get lonely?"

"Sure. But there are ways a man can relieve his loneliness."

Dinah blushed. "That don't exactly make you less lonely. Just . . ." She was too embarrassed to continue.

"Depends on how you look at it, I reckon. Besides, we're discussin' you and your future, not me and my past. Do you think you can trust Lacy's husband?"

"I think so."

"First thing in the mornin', wire her. If she knows about your pa, tell her you're fleein' him and need a place to settle while you think things out. If she doesn't, tell her your beau left you, and you just want to get away for a spell."

"I figure she does."

"Good. That makes it simpler. And make sure you keep that pretty little mouth of yours shut. Same goes for Lacy and her husband."

Dinah's face brightened, then immediately fell. "I ain't got the money to send a telegram, let alone afford transportation to get there."

Pike reached into a pocket and slid a gold double eagle across the table. "That's for the telegram. Money for a stage or train, whichever goes up that way, will be there when the time comes."

"I'll have no way to pay you back. No way to find you either, if I did get some money."

"Ain't no concern of yours. I ain't askin' for a return of the money, nor do I expect it."

"But . . ."

"I owe it to you, Dinah. I was hornswoggled." He gritted his teeth. "If I hadn't been, I would've never done what I did. I ain't a cruel man, and I don't like having been made a fool of."

Dinah rushed into the restaurant where Pike was sitting at lunch. "She said I was welcome. Lacy said she was happy to have me!" Her joy overrode her anger at Pike.

"That's good. Now sit and eat. Afterward, we'll see about getting' you there."

Dinah ordered, but she was so excited she could barely eat. Pike would have been amused if he wasn't still so ashamed. Soon

58

enough, though, they checked out the train and stage schedules. A train was leaving for Denver the next morning. From there, Dinah could catch another train to Boulder.

Pike paid for her ticket, and when they were at dinner, he quietly and surreptitiously handed her three hundred dollars.

"I can't take that," she said, not making any effort to give it back.

"Yes, you can. Like I said, I owe you. I got enough. I might even get more from your pa."

"You're going back to see him?" Dinah asked, suddenly frightened.

"Reckon so."

"You're gonna tell him where I've gone, aren't you?" She was very afraid now and began to rise.

"Sit down," Pike ordered. When she did, he said, "I'm not gonna do any such thing. He offered me five hundred dollars to bring you back. I figure that even if I couldn't do that, he still owes me for the time and effort."

"What're you gonna tell him?"

"You're dead." He grinned.

"What?"

"I caught up to them fellas, and I learned that they had killed you a few days before and buried you somewhere. Told me they didn't know exactly where, so your bones are restin' in a mountain meadow somewhere. Or been eaten by wolves. Either way, you're gone forever."

Dinah was silent for a bit, mulling that over. Then she grinned. "You're a devious man, ain't you, Brodie Pike?"

"Yep."

Brodie Pike knocked loudly on Asa Wilkins's door. When Wilkins answered, he snapped, "Where's my daughter?"

"Dead. Where's my money?"

"Where's her body?"

"Out there somewhere. Those boys killed her, and I buried her in a meadow up in the mountains. Where's my money?"

"If she's dead, you didn't bring her home to me, so you don't get any money." He started to shut the door.

Pike smashed the door inward with both hands, sending Wilkins staggering. Pike stepped in, grabbed Wilkins's shirtfront, and slammed him against the wall. "I don't think you understand me, Mr. Wilkins," Pike said, letting his anger at this man for duping him rise. "You sent me to find your daughter. I did."

"I hired you to bring her home to me," Wilkins said, voice a little shaky. "You didn't do so, so you don't get any money."

"I rode long and hard, chasin' men who you said were killers and desperate outlaws. Killed all three of 'em," he said, twisting the truth a bit. "All because you lied to me. Then I buried your daughter. I deserve that money, and I ain't leavin' here 'til I get my rightful due."

Pike could see in Wilkins's eyes that the wheels were turning in his head. He didn't know Pike knew of his abuse of Dinah and figured that if she were dead, he was in no danger of being discovered.

"Sure," Wilkins finally said. "Sure. You deserve it. I'll go in the parlor there where I keep some money."

"I will escort you, just to make sure you're gettin' money and not a gun. Lead on." Pike pulled him away from the wall and shoved him forward.

Wilkins knelt and reached under a sofa. Pike drew a Colt and cocked it. Wilkins tensed but pulled a tin box out and turned, still kneeling, to face Pike, the box in front of him. He opened it and pulled out some greenbacks, then stood and handed them to Pike with a nervous hand. "There's three hundred and fifty bucks. It's all I got."

The rage in Pike rose even higher at the thought of being deceived by this man again. "You son of a bitch," he growled. He slid his six-gun back into the holster and then smashed Wilkins in the face, knocking him onto the sofa. The dollars scattered as Wilkins flew backward. "Where's the rest?"

"There ain't no more. I just told you."

"You were gonna cheat me out of a hundred fifty bucks even if I brought her back?"

"I . . . I . . . I thought you were gonna kill those men and collect the reward."

"Get off your ass, pick up the money, and give it to me." When Wilkins did, Pike stood there seething for a minute. "How many horses you got?"

"Three?" There was a question in his voice.

"Got paper and a pen?"

"On that table," Wilkins said, pointing.

"Write me out a bill of sale for all three horses."

"You can't take my horses," Wilkins sputtered.

"Hell I can't. It'll make up what you owe me."

"But . . ."

Pike hit him in the face again. "Do it, you son of a bitch, or I'll shoot you dead and take the horses."

Holding his nose, trying to stanch the blood, Wilkins did as he was told. He handed the paper to Pike, who swiftly read it.

He stuck the paper in his shirt pocket, along with the money, then pulled out one of his revolvers. "Now that I got this paper, I legally own those horses. I should just kill you and be on my way." He thumbed back the hammer, fighting hard to not do just that. He aimed, then suddenly fired.

Wilkins screamed as the bullet tore an inch-deep grove in the flesh where the shoulder and neck join.

"I suggest you treat that by yourself. If you do go to town to see a doc, you'd best tell him — or any lawman who shows an interest — that you accidentally shot yourself. If you send a law dog after me, I'll kill him, then come back here and kill you. Understand?"

"Yes," Wilkins said weakly.

"I also suggest you not try to cheat anyone else you do business with." Pike thought of hitting Wilkins again, but he turned and walked out instead. After rounding up the three horses, he rode off with them, heading for a town some distance from Arvada to sell the animals.

CHAPTER 5

Brodie Pike rode back into Graystone shortly before dark and went straight to the livery. After turning in the wagon and horse, he headed for the hotel. The proprietor was not elated at Pike's return, but he accepted it.

After putting his things in his room, he headed to a restaurant. The meal he had had at the small ranch house had been tasty but not enough to fill him. When he finished, he debated whether he should stop by a saloon. He decided he would, but he silently vowed he would not stick his nose in anyone else's altercation. He did choose another saloon, though.

He had a beer and two shots of whiskey but no trouble, which pleased him. A good night's sleep did all the more. And after breakfast in the morning, he went to Marshal Uriah Haney's office.

The lawman was startled, and fear and

then annoyance flickered across his face. "What the hell do you want?" he growled, hoping that would disguise his nervousness.

"You heard anything of Jethro Harker and his boys in these parts lately?"

"Never heard of him."

"That so? Then you're either a liar, or you're dumber than a pile of dirt. Likely, I think, both."

"I don't think I —"

"It's certain you don't think."

"Dammit, I don't like bein' called a liar or stupid."

"Well, then stop lyin' and actin' stupid, you damn fool. If you hadn't heard of Harker, you probably wouldn't be in that chair. He's one of the biggest rustlers in the Territory when he and his boys ain't robbin' banks and killin' folks. Your bosses will know that. So, you heard of them lately in these parts?"

"If they were, the range detectives would've taken care of them by now." At Pike's baleful look, he added, "Not in this county, no. Over in Sharpsville in Grant County, though, I heard there was a bank robbery and some cattle thefts. I ain't sure, but Dex Carver, he's the Grant County sheriff, says it was them."

"See, that wasn't so hard, Marshal. You

learn to be a little more open to folks and a lot less hostile, you'll get through life a lot easier."

Haney grunted, then asked, "You leavin' town now?"

"I was plannin' to." He grinned insolently. " 'Course, if you'll miss my company, I'd be glad to stay around a while."

Haney managed to knock the shocked look off his face after about two seconds and growled, "Get out."

"Is that any way to treat an old friend?"

"Get out!"

Laughing, Pike turned and walked away, ignoring the "And don't come back!" Haney threw at him as he slipped out the door.

As he was heading back to the hotel to get his belongings, Pike was stopped by a well-dressed man. "A moment of your time, Mr. Pike?" the man asked.

"Only a moment."

"My name is Ulysses Hungerford, and I'd like to talk to you a bit."

"Not interested."

"It might be worth your while."

"Is that a threat?"

"My word, no. Just some conversation that might hold some interest for you."

Pike stood there, considering the request. He was pretty sure he knew what Hungerford wanted to talk about, and he really didn't want to hear it. On the other hand, it might give him some insight into what Hungerford was thinking concerning the McAllisters and the others. It might not help any, but it was worth a few minutes. He nodded. "Speak your piece."

"A public street isn't the place to discuss important matters."

"What do you suggest?"

"Buckskin County Cattlemen's club."

Pike looked Hungerford over. The cattleman was above medium height, though not by much, and stout. His suit was high quality, the open jacket revealing a vest — silk, Pike thought. His bowler hat, too, was silk. He had a florid face that radiated slyness, fronted by a wide, bulbous nose. "Lead on," Pike finally said.

The building two blocks away was as ostentatious as he had thought it would be. It stood out from the rest of the town, especially since it had no other buildings close to it. Inside was just as pretentious, with a small bar to the left, a dining room on the right near the back, and couches, overstuffed chairs, and fine tables scattered around the main room. A staircase led to several rooms in a U shape. Hungerford plopped his plumpness down in a soft, cushiony leather chair and indicated another across the small table from him.

Pike looked around and spotted a straight-back wood chair with a thick brocade seat. He grabbed it, brought it over next to the plush chair, and sat in it.

"Something wrong with comfort, Mr. Pike?"

"Nope. But if I was to need to protect myself, gettin' up out of one of those chairs would slow me down too much."

"You feel threatened here?"

"Just bein' cautious."

"Good way to be, I reckon," Hungerford agreed.

"It's how I've managed to survive. So, what did you want to talk to me about?"

"I understand you visited the McAllisters and their relatives yesterday."

"Whether I did or didn't is no concern of yours."

"Everything that happens in Buckskin County is my business."

"Have a mighty high opinion of yourself, don't you?"

"Yes. As head of the Buckskin County Cattlemen's Association, anything that happens here is of importance to me, and is therefore my business." His voice oozed arrogance.

"You seem to have a misconception as to your importance in my life and activities."

Hungerford was shocked. "Why, you insignificant . . ." He drew a deep breath and calmed himself. "It seems we have gotten off on the wrong foot here. Let me start again. The cattlemen have been experiencing more than a little rustling. Small-timers like the McAllisters and their relations are among the worst."

"How does that affect me?"

"The association has hired a few range detectives to stop the rustling."

"I'm acquainted with them," Pike said, sarcasm thick in his voice.

"So I've heard. Takes a man with big stones to face down those four. Especially for someone you apparently didn't know."

Pike shrugged. "Didn't like the odds."

"I could use a man like you, Mr. Pike. That's why I see it as my business whether you visited those people."

"My decision about whether I'll work for you has nothin' to do with whether I visited 'those folks,' as you call 'em."

"I beg to differ. If you did visit those folks, I need to know why before I offer you a chance to join the range detectives."

"Why?"

"Because if you did visit them, you may

have hired on with them, though I can't see how they would be able to afford it, despite the number of cattle they've rustled."

Pike was silent for a few moments, then said, "Doesn't matter whether I went there or not. I don't hire on with anyone, and that will include you."

"Working for the association has some attractive benefits: good money, decent place to stay, prestige." He gave an unctuous smile. "And power."

"Such work has drawbacks, too."

"Oh?"

"Harassin' innocent folks is one of 'em. Worse would be killin' 'em 'cause you claim they're rustlin' your cattle without any proof."

"Ah, but we have proof."

"I doubt that, Mr. Hungerford. I think you just want the land those folks have settled on and are willin' to hire a passel of gunmen to intimidate 'em, harass 'em, and kill 'em so you can get it."

"My detectives haven't killed any of them," Hungerford said defensively.

"They killed Edgar Dunn."

"You can't prove that."

"Nope, but you and I both know it's the truth."

"That's a strong accusation."

"Only made to you. I have no plans on makin' it to anyone else."

"A wise thought."

Pike glared at Hungerford, taking a moment to thrust away the desire to hit the man. "You ever consider offerin' a decent price for their land and all the rest?"

"Why would I do that?"

"Make it easier on everyone. They get a fair price so they can move on and have enough to start over somewhere else. You get your land, you save money by no longer havin' to hire a herd of thugs, and you stop the rustlin' if there really is any. All for a reasonable amount of money."

"That would also give others of their ilk ideas, and we'd face a regular dose of extortion by rustlers and homesteaders."

"Seems unlikely, since all the homesteaders and small ranchers would be gone. It ain't likely that others'd move in."

"Ah, but some would when they heard they can hold up the association for exorbitant amounts of money. Better we should drive them out. Not only would it relieve the association members of a passel of rustlers, it would also send a strong message to any others who might try to extort our members."

Pike shook his head at the man's audac-

71

ity, though he had run into such men before. "You're even more arrogant and stupid than I originally thought."

"You son of a bitch. How dare you, a no-account saddle tramp of a gunman, speak to me like that."

"You also seem to have a misconception that I will listen to such claptrap from a goat-humper like you."

Pike stood and took a few steps before Hungerford roared, "Sit down!"

Pike turned back. "One more word to me in that tone, Mr. Hungerford, and I will shoot that skunk turd behind the door before putting a bullet in that portly face of yours."

"You just watch your back, Pike."

"You do the same, Hungerford. You have a lot more to worry about than I do. You'd do well not to trust those hired guns of yours."

CHAPTER 6

Before long, Pike was riding out of town, heading toward the mountains. He was traveling light, hoping he could take care of the business of running down Harker's gang quickly. But first he had a stop to make.

He rode to the McAllister ranchland and found Matt McAllister. They pulled their horses up side by side, facing each other.

"Come to join after all, Mr. Pike?" the rancher asked.

Pike shook his head. "Nope. I'm headin' out on the trail of a band of outlaws I've been chasin' a while. I just wanted to come by and tell you I had a talk with Hungerford this mornin'."

"Oh?" McAllister's shoulders tightened. "Hired you on, did he?"

"You don't really think that."

"No. Just worried."

"Well, you should be worried, but not about that. He did say he'd like to hire me,

73

but I told him the same thing I told you: I don't hire my gun out."

"Then why are you here?"

"Give you a warnin'. When I talked to him, I mentioned that it might be good if he bought you out. He wouldn't even hear of it. Thinks it'll cause him problems with others."

"So there's no sense in goin' to town and tryin' to have somebody approach him." It was more of a statement than a question.

"No. Though there's still the possibility of tryin' to get word to one of the other association officials."

"That won't work, will it?"

"Doubt it."

"How do I know you're tellin' me the truth?"

"You don't, other than I tell you I am. Believe it or don't."

"I do," McAllister said with a nod. "So, we're in the same pickle we've been in for a spell."

"Reckon you are."

"Well, thanks for lettin' me know, Mr. Pike." He leaned forward a little and held out his hand.

Pike shook it. "Good luck to you and everyone in your family, Mr. McAllister." He turned his horse and trotted off with an uneasy feeling settling over him.

Two days later, Pike rode into Sharpsville. As soon as he stabled his horse and found a room, he wandered off in search of the sheriff's office. It was locked. While he stood there contemplating his next move, a man stopped a few feet away. "Sheriff's over at the Star Point." He pointed.

"He frequent the place?"

"Yep, but he mostly drinks coffee. He ain't drunk, if that's what you're askin'."

"It was. Obliged." He headed down the street and entered the saloon. It was typical of the area — walnut bar along the left wall, with a fully stocked back bar, a painting of a lounging nude woman centered amid the towers of bottles, and a number of tables for drinking patrons, several of which were occupied. At the rear were a roulette wheel, two faro tables, and three tables for poker and other games of chance. Pike was a little surprised that it was only one story since there were several working girls roaming the room, so he figured there were cribs out back.

It took but a few moments to spot the sheriff — a tall, slender fellow with long, wavy black hair and a magnificent mustache that drooped well past his chin. Pike walked up. "Mind if I join you, Sheriff?"

"Why?"

"Like to talk to you."

"What about?"

"Jethro Harker."

Sheriff Dex Carver's eyes raised in surprise. "What's your name, mister?"

"Brodie Pike."

"Sit, Mr. Pike. Something to drink?"

"Coffee'll do."

Carver waved at the bartender, and a moment later, Pike had coffee in front of him. "So why Sharpsville in your search for Harker?"

"Marshal over in Graystone said you'd had some trouble here with him and his boys."

"Marshal Haney wired me about you. Said you were trouble."

"I can be when prodded. And Haney didn't impress me much."

Carver suddenly grinned. "Haney's a horse's ass for certain." He reached across the table and shook Pike's hand. "So, you're looking for Harker and his whole gang by yourself?"

Pike shrugged and offered a crooked grin. "I've always worked alone."

"When Haney wired me, I did some checking of my own. Seems you're mighty good at what you do, but takin' on Harker

76

and all seven of his boys alone? You're out of your mind."

Pike chuckled. "There have been many times I'd have agreed with that. This is one of 'em."

"Least you have enough sense to realize it."

"So, what kind of trouble did you have with Harker's bunch?"

"Several ranches reported a few dozen head of cattle stolen, and they hit banks in Rockville and Mineral City. Got away with more than fifty thousand from those two."

"Pretty good haul."

"Indeed it was."

"Both places in the county?" When Carver nodded, Pike asked, "I assume you chased after 'em."

The lawman's face darkened with anger and grief as he nodded. "Rode out as soon as I heard. Picked up a posse in Rockville and rode hard. Bastards killed one deputy and two townsmen in the posse. At that point, we returned home. Posse members weren't keen on continuing on. To be truthful, neither was I. The men who were killed were all friends."

"No shame in that. In fact, it makes a heap of sense."

Carver just grunted. It galled him that

he'd had to do it; that it had been the only sensible thing to do under the circumstances. But he didn't like it, and he never would.

"I get the sense you'd still like to go after 'em and take care of business."

"It's that obvious?" Carver asked a little sourly.

Pike nodded. He sipped his coffee, then said quietly, "You could ride along with me."

Carver thought that over, then shook his head. "Too many duties in the county. Besides, if what I heard was true, they're out of my jurisdiction."

"You could take leave."

"County Commission would never condone it."

A slow grin spread over Pike's face. "You could tell the commissioners that you got word Harker and his boys were spotted in the county again and you need to check it out."

Once again, the lawman sat quietly and contemplated that. Then his great mustache rose, and a smile slid across his face. "By golly, that's a grand idea, Mr. Pike. Yes, sir, I do believe you — or someone else — just brought me word that Harker and his boys were spotted in the little town of Elk Pond in the northwest part of the county. It is my sworn duty to check that story out."

He raised his coffee mug and clinked it against Pike's. "You'll be ready at first light, Mr. Pike?"

"I certainly will, Sheriff."

Dawn was just pinking the sky when Pike entered the livery stable. Carver's horse was saddled, and the sheriff was loading supplies on a mule.

"Plannin' on bein' out a while?" Pike asked with a grin.

"Hope not, but best to be prepared."

"Amen to that," Pike agreed as he began saddling his own horse. As he attached a special scabbard containing a second rifle besides his Winchester to the saddle, Carver asked, "What in hell's that?"

"Sharps .52-caliber with scope," Pike said.

"Sniper rifle?"

Pike nodded. "Used it in the war."

"Must be a hell of a weapon."

"It is."

Minutes later, they rode out of town, heading due west. "Since this whole plan was a ruse, I suppose we're not really plannin' to go to Elk Pond?"

"Correct. I chose Elk Pond to tell the commissioners last night because it's a pissant spot at the far end of the county.

Nobody's gonna think of checkin' up there."

"So, where are we headin'?"

"Mining town called Hopeful. Seems they were headed in that direction. Place was boomin' last time I checked, so they might've thought it'd be easy pickin's for 'em. If we don't pick up a trail there, we'll head to Wolfsburg, seat of Jefferson County. The sheriff there, fella named Ken Sorenson, will know something if there's anything to be known."

"Why not stop there first?"

"Hopeful's closer."

Late on the day after they left Sharpsville, they arrived in Hopeful and learned that Harker's bunch had indeed raided the mining town. The outlaws killed two miners, wounded half a dozen others, and stole an estimated twenty thousand dollars in gold dust and nuggets before riding off, taking two unwilling prostitutes with them.

"Nobody chased 'em?" Pike asked the de facto mayor, a short, skinny man everyone called Goldfoot.

"We got no law here, mister. Not even a vigilance committee. We're just simple miners. Ain't likely to face down a horde of killers like them boys. No, sir, ain't likely to a'tall. We can dig us more dust and nuggets, but we can't grow back Mouse and Stringbean, who was killed by them fellers."

"Nope, wouldn't expect you to chase such hoodlums. Just wonderin', as I didn't know you had no law."

"Which way did they head?" Carver asked.

"South out of town. Where they went after that, we got no idea."

"When?"

"Week, maybe eight days ago."

Carver looked at Pike and said, "No rush." Pike nodded, and Carver asked Goldfoot, "Mind if we stay in town for the night? Could use a hot meal and see that the horses get some rest."

"Be delighted. Hopeful's a rough place, but we do have one hotel that ain't half bad. Mrs. Pinewood, the owner's wife, cooks up some mean pork chops. And the livery's pretty good."

"Obliged."

The service, while not exemplary, was as good as advertised, and satisfied with a good supper, a good night's rest, and a fine breakfast, Pike and Carver rode south the next morning. A mile outside town, they started sweeping from left to right, widening their search, looking for signs of the outlaws' passage.

Around midmorning, they found them. They moved faster, now heading southwest.

"Anything out here?" Pike asked.

"Couple small towns if I remember right. Mining places, so they might've folded up already. Doubt they offer much interest to Harker, though they're such nasty bastards, they just might raid those places for the hell of it. After that, if they turn west just past the second place, they'll be on a line for Wolfsburg."

"Know the marshal there?"

Carver nodded. "Old feller named Lyles. Not much use, but not a bad man."

"Kurt Sorenson is the Jefferson County sheriff, you said?"

Carver nodded.

"Like him?"

"Don't like him, don't dislike him. He's mostly competent, though a bit reluctant to chase bad men at times. Not sure if he'll have chased Harker if his bunch has been through this way."

"Reckon we'll see."

CHAPTER 7

The first mining town, which had no name, was abandoned. The second, simply called "Here," had but a few people left.

"Band of cutthroats rode through the other day," one man said. "Killed Elmer, burned down most of our shacks, stole what little dust we had, and rode off laughing. Most of the fellers here left right after that. Me and these few others decided to stick around."

"Why?" Pike asked.

"There's still gold to be found hereabouts, and I doubt them outlaw fellers will be back. Ain't worth their while."

"Which way were they headed?" Carver asked.

"West. Didn't seem in any hurry, though."

"Obliged."

Pike and Carver headed out again, moving a bit faster. If Harker's men were moving leisurely and it had been only a few days since they had raided Here, the two men thought they might catch the outlaws before the band reached Wolfsburg.

The trail was easy enough to follow most of the time, but Pike and Carver did not catch them before they arrived in Wolfsburg at midday two days later since they had taken the time to bury the two prostitutes Harker's gang had taken from Hopeful. They stopped at the Jefferson County sheriff's office, tied their horses to the hitching rail, and went inside.

A weary-looking deputy glanced up and asked, "What can I do for you, fellas?"

"Where's Sheriff Sorenson?" Carver asked.

"Boneyard."

"What'n hell happened to him?" a shocked Carver asked.

"Killed leadin' a posse after some bad men day before yesterday."

"Harker's bunch?"

"Yep. Robbed the bank and lit out. Kurt and I got up a posse and lit out after 'em. Couple hours later, we came back with Kurt shot full of holes. The outlaw scum ambushed us. Kurt was out front, and they blasted the hell out of him. Me and a couple of the men managed to grab his body durin' a lull in the shootin', and we all hightailed it back here."

"What about the town marshal?"

"What about him?"

"He do anything?"

The deputy snorted out a short laugh. "Chicken-hearted bastard said that as soon as they got out of town, they weren't his problem."

"Nice of him," Pike said dryly.

"Yeah." The deputy sighed.

"You're the new sheriff, then?"

"Reckon so. Sorry, name's Sam Gilpin."

Carver introduced himself and Pike, and handshakes were exchanged all around. "Plannin' to do anything about Harker?"

"Hell, no. Ain't a man in Wolfsburg who'll go out on a posse with me now, and I sure as hell ain't goin' after 'em by myself."

Carver gave Pike a questioning look, and the bounty hunter nodded. "How's about you join us two in the hunt?" the former asked.

Some of the tiredness lifted from Gilpin's face. "You're joshin', right?"

"Nope. The two of us might be enough to handle all of 'em, but it sure won't hurt to have another gun along."

"How do you know I'm any good? I could be a burden to you."

"Doubt it. Kurt Sorenson might not've

been the best sheriff around, but he was a steady hand and mostly took his job seriously. If he hired you as a deputy, I reckon he had a reason."

Gilpin sat thinking for more than a minute, then he grinned. "What the hell," he said. "It might be crazy, but I'm in." He grew somber. "Maybe I can find some justice for Kurt."

"Dawn tomorrow?"

"I'll be ready."

"What'd you do with your badge, Sam?" Carver asked.

"Gave it to one of the county officials," Gilpin said. "Told him I was leavin' town. Didn't tell him why, just that I hadn't been elected, so I didn't have to keep the job. I think he thinks I'm a coward, runnin' off because Kurt got killed."

"That doesn't bother you?"

"Some, but not enough to worry about, or enough for me to explain to him and his kind. If I come out of this all right and decide to come back here, they won't be able to call me a coward."

"No family?"

"Nope. Was married a while, but diphtheria took her a couple years ago."

"Sorry to hear that."

Gilpin shrugged. "It's in the past."

They were silent as they finished saddling their horses and loading supplies on the mule, lost in their memories of loved ones now gone.

"Which way?" Carver finally asked.

"They were headed southwest when we caught up to 'em."

"Nothin' out there as far as I can recall."

"A ranch or two is all. They might try raidin' 'em, but I don't think so. I think they're headin' for a hideout out there to rest up 'til things calm down, then head somewhere and spend their loot."

"Where would they be holin' up?" Pike asked.

"Plenty of canyons, most of 'em hard to find. Used to be some folks tried to make a livin' out there, damn fools, 'til Indians drove 'em out."

"Then southwest we go," Carver said. "I just hope we can catch 'em before they get to one of those places. I'd hate like hell to have to search every damn canyon we come across, lookin' for 'em."

"Amen to that," Pike said. "Let's move."

A couple miles outside of town, the three split, with Pike riding out to the left and Carver to the right as they sought signs of Harker's passage. Around midmorning,

Pike dismounted and found some tracks amid a stand of cottonwoods along a small stream. He fired his pistol, then loosened the horse's cinch to let it breathe as he waited.

Gilpin showed up ten minutes later, and Carver about the same after that. "What'd you find?"

Pike showed the other two. "Looks like they camped here two or three nights ago."

"Sure it's them?" Carver asked.

"Yep. Saw several hoofprints we've been following and the stubs of a couple cigars of the kind we know they favor. And they're drivin' a few cattle with 'em. I found a spot upstream a bit where they butchered a steer. Judgin' by the refuse lyin' around, I'd say they were here for two nights, maybe three."

"Don't seem too worried about bein' followed, then," Gilpin said.

"That's my thinkin'."

"Then let's get movin' again," Carver said.

"We ain't that close, so no need to rush ahead without thinkin'," Pike said. "Your horses need water and a little rest since we'll push hard once we do get back on the trail."

Carver nodded. They unsaddled the horses but did not unload the mule and led the animals down to the stream to drink their fill, then hobbled them and let them graze along with Pike's sorrel. The men sat and ate some of the cold chicken they had gotten from the miners in Here and drank from the cold stream.

In about three-quarters of an hour, they were saddled up and back on the trail. Having little trouble following the tracks, they were able to push hard and make up some distance. They stopped as dusk was fading into night. The trio had already fallen into a routine in taking on the chores — all three gathered firewood, then Pike unsaddled the horses, Carver unloaded the mule, and Gilpin built a fire and made coffee and got the deer Carver had shot that afternoon cooking.

As they ate, Carver asked, "You have any idea where exactly those snakes might be goin', Sam?"

"I might, but I ain't sure yet. I should be able to tell tomorrow, dependin' on where the tracks take us." After a few moments, he asked, "So, how'd you two get involved in this?"

"I've been chasin' 'em for a while now," Pike said. "Didn't seem to be getting much closer to 'em 'til I hit Sharpsville."

"Which is where he hoodwinked me into joinin' him," Carver said with a chuckle.

"Kind of the way you two hornswoggled

me into accompanyin' you," Gilpin said, grinning.

"Didn't take much convincin' for either you or me," Carver said.

"True. Well, boys, time for me to hit the hay."

The other two agreed, and all turned in.

Just after noon the next day, Gilpin called a halt. He and Pike dismounted and checked the ground for tracks. "Still headin' southwest," the former said.

"So, what's that mean?" Carver asked, dismounting and joining them.

"Likely means they're headin' for Stinkin' Goat Canyon, which I thought might be the one. It's a narrow canyon, maybe a mile or a bit longer, with a small stream cutting through it. Plenty of game. Entry is guarded by thick stands of trees and a tight passage, but it mostly opens once you get inside. Cliffs aren't more than fifty or sixty feet high and are rugged sandstone."

"Sounds like they'll have it mighty comfortable in there," Pike said.

"And it might be hard to flush 'em out. Maybe one of us should ride around to the other end to block off any retreat they might try when the other two hit 'em from the front," Carver said.

Gilpin grinned. "One thing I hadn't mentioned — it's a box canyon. No way out except the way in."

"That'll make it a heap easier to take 'em on," Pike said.

"How far is it?" Carver asked.

"Half a day's ride or thereabout," Gilpin said. "I reckon we can take our lunch here, let the horses drink and eat, and then move on. We can camp for the night just outside the mouth of the canyon."

Pike and Carver nodded. They didn't waste much time, but they did make a small fire to brew coffee to go with the cold venison they had cooked the night before. With full bellies and rested horses, they pressed on slowly, in no real hurry now that they knew their destination and that they would not be heading into the canyon this day.

It took less time than they had figured, and well before dusk, they swung into a thick copse of cottonwoods and willows a quarter-mile from the entrance to the canyon.

"Sure we won't be spotted, bein' so close?" Pike asked.

"Not unless they've decided to make their home fifty yards from here," Gilpin said. "I reckon they're well into the canyon."

Pike and Carver accepted that and began setting up their camp.

CHAPTER 8

They left the mule behind, hobbled so it could feed but not wander too far off. They also left the supplies, except for canteens, extra ammunition, and some jerky.

"Not takin' that fancy rifle of yours, Brodie?"

"It's good for long-range shootin', but I suspect that won't be the case here."

They wove their way through thick stands of trees and then a passage between cliffs that sprang up suddenly. It was so narrow the men had to file through it one at a time, with little clearance on either side.

The canyon opened up to about fifty yards wide. Water spilled through a small crevice in the rock wall to their left, forming a small, gently flowing stream. They moved slowly, watching for sign of where the outlaws were staying.

It wasn't long in coming. Gilpin pulled up and pointed. It took only a few moments for his two companions to see the thin swirl of smoke rising above the canyon around a twist in the cliff walls.

"Wouldn't it be good to have one of us head up along the rim of the canyon an' look down on those skunks?" Carver asked.

"Can't. At the top of the cliffs all the way around, the rocks slope sharply for some distance. No chance of gettin' close to the rim."

"You're just full of good news, ain't you?"

"Could be worse."

"Think they'll have lookouts?" Pike asked.

"Doubt it, though I don't know them well enough to know their thinkin'. I reckon they figure no one's gonna be lookin' for 'em in here, so they'll expect to be safe."

"How do we play this?" Pike asked.

"I expect it'd be best if one of us was to get up close to 'em and see how things look," Gilpin said. "Once we know how they're set up, we can plan."

"And who would this scout be?"

"Reckon me," Gilpin said. "I know a little about this canyon, and you boys don't know anything about it."

Pike and Carver nodded. "How far do we go before you split off on your own?" Pike asked.

"I think there's three more big twists

along the way. Judgin' from the smoke, I figure they're at the far end, so we can go almost to that last one."

"All right, Sam, lead the way," Pike said.

They moved slowly, careful to make no moves that might attract attention if the outlaws were out and about. The distance was not far, and in less than half an hour, they reached a spot that Gilpin thought was close enough. They stopped in a small grove of oaks along the stream. They loosened their cinches and let the horses drink. Then Gilpin tightened the strap and mounted. "Be back soon's I can," he said before riding off.

As noon came and went and Gilpin had not returned, Carver began to get fidgety. He paced, then sat, then paced some more. Finally, Pike, still sitting with his back against a rock, told him, "Sit down, Dex. You're annoyin' the hell out of me."

"Why ain't he back yet? Maybe they caught him."

"Ain't heard any gunfire. If they caught him, they were quiet about it, and he was mighty quiet going with them. I reckon he would've gotten off one shot before they roped him in."

"How can you be so patient just sittin'

there? Don't you have any nerves?"

"Same number as any man. I've learned over the years to control 'em. It doesn't do any good for you to let them get the better of you. It clouds your thinkin' and wastes your energy pacin' around. Sit and conserve your strength for when it's needed."

"It ain't so easy for some of us," Carver said, plopping down.

Pike grinned. "Never said it was. Took me a long while to figure it out. Just sit there and relax. Think about how pleasurable it'll be to be back in Wolfsburg in a few days, sippin' a cold, foamy beer and maybe sportin' with some of the ladies at whatever nice brothel there is in town."

"If we get back," he grumbled.

"Damn, you're a gloomy fella, Dex. Attitude like that'll make your chances of that comin' true pretty strong. You need to go into a battle certain you'll be the victor. Thinkin' otherwise almost guarantees you'll end up on the wrong end of things, especially if it's before the shootin' even starts."

"You always think like that?"

"Mostly. Comes a time now and again when things look mighty bleak and I start thinkin' this is the end, but even then, something inside tells me I'm gonna win. Been right so far."

"I think you're a heap different than most fellas, Mr. Pike. Not another fella I know can face a showdown with a passel of outlaws with such composure."

Pike shrugged, rather embarrassed by the praise. He pulled his hat down a little to cover his eyes and dozed.

Carver sat there shaking his head. He had come across some interesting men in his life, but never one quite as perplexing and seemingly fearless as Brodie Pike. He tried to emulate him, with a little success.

Gilpin's arrival woke Pike from his nap, and he stood. Carver waited anxiously as Gilpin dismounted and led his horse to the stream. "Well?" Carver finally demanded.

"Well, what?" Gilpin asked with a look of innocence on his face.

"Damn, if you and Brodie ain't the most exasperatin' fellas I ever met. You know damn well what."

Gilpin grinned. "Gee, Dex, can't a guy even have a minute to rub his saddle-sore ass before you start interrogatin' him?"

"Jumpin' Jehoshaphat, you're a maddening fella, Sam. Go ahead and scratch your ass, then tell us."

Gilpin did so with a chuckle, then said, "Well, I moseyed on down the west side of the river for fifty yards or so, then I crossed on over to the . . ."

"By all the saints," Carver bellowed, throwing his hat at Gilpin, "get to the point!"

Both Pike and Gilpin were laughing now, further exasperating Carver. It took a couple of minutes for the latter to regain his breath so he could speak.

"I think all eight of 'em are there. They got a cabin right up against the back wall of the canyon, another tall, straight cliff more than a hundred feet tall. No trails going up it, so they're boxed in. There's a small corral to the left. I saw ten horses and a couple of steers in it. A privy that doesn't look too substantial is on the other side. Window on each side of the front door. I couldn't get around to the side, so I don't know if there're windows there."

"Any cover for us to move up to 'em?" Pike asked.

"Not a hell of a lot, no. A line of trees along the stream leadin' up to the corral. An oak here and there in front, but not enough cover to get close enough and hide behind while we try to draw 'em out."

"Can you get all three of us as close as you were?"

"Reckon so, Brodie. You just plannin' to attack?"

"Nope. Just want to get to a place where I can get the lay of the land. Maybe if I see just what we're facin', I can come up with a plan."

"Makes sense, but it'll have to wait a bit. I got an empty belly that needs fillin' and a horse that needs some rest."

"Take what time you need, Sam," Pike said. He looked at Carver. "You still jumpy, Dex?"

"Not as much, knowin' we're gonna see some action soon. Though not soon enough."

Gilpin was ready quickly, and they mounted and rode off single file. They stopped at the last stand of cottonwoods. Ahead of them was the cabin and almost a hundred yards of empty space broken only by a few scattered trees and some boulders, none of which was large enough to provide much cover.

"Doesn't look good, does it?" Gilpin said more than asked.

"Can't say I disagree with that," Pike said.

"I don't see much of a problem," Carver said. "I say we just wait 'til dark, then slip on down there and burn 'em out. When they run out, we can see 'em fine by the light of the burnin' cabin, and we can gun 'em down easy."

"How?" Pike asked. "Slip down there with a handful of matches and hope to get something going? Start a fire here and carry a torch across that field? You'll be spotted sure as hell before you get halfway across."

"If they're even payin' attention, which ain't likely, considerin' they think they're safe here."

"Good chance of that," Gilpin said after thinking it over.

"One other problem with that idea," Pike said, glancing up at the sky. "Looks like it'll be rainin' in an hour or so."

Carver and Gilpin looked up, and each shook his head. "Damn," Carver muttered for both of them.

"Any other ideas, then?" Gilpin asked.

"None that come to mind. Looks like our options are mighty limited."

"I reckon we could wait 'til just before dawn, ride down there, and shoot 'em as they come out to use the privy."

"You think they'll all come out together to take a leak?" Pike said with a small laugh. "We gun down one or two of 'em who come out, the rest'll sit there nice and comfortable in their cabin, shootin' at us while we're standin' there out in the open, makin' fine targets."

"Damn, you are a ray of sunshine, Brodie," Carver said.

"Makes me popular."

"Not around here, it doesn't."

Pike shrugged. "We'll figure out something."

"Sure we . . ."

"Hush," Pike snapped, shutting him up.

Before either of the other two could say anything, Pike held a finger to his lips. A moment later, they heard the snapping of twigs coming from the trees across the stream. The three silently drew their revolvers and drifted apart, moving away from the horses and stopping behind trees, waiting and watching.

Minutes later, a man peered out of the oaks, attracted by the jingle of bits and the snuffling of the horses. He peered around a bit, then spun and rushed back into the trees.

"Damn," Pike muttered, figuring the man was heading for his own horse farther back in the trees. Pike shoved his pistol away as he dashed across the stream and plunged into the forest, angling in the direction of the cabin. He soon spotted the outlaw mounting his horse and trying to whip it into a run. He ran a little faster, bounded off a flat boulder a foot high, and launched himself at the horseman. He tackled the man, and both tumbled to the ground.

Pike was up first and kicked the man in the chin, dazing him, then stomped on the man's stomach, keeping him from breathing well and thus preventing him from shouting an alarm. Leaving him for a moment, he got the man's horse, whose reins had gotten tangled in a chokecherry bush. Pike managed to calm the animal, then whacked the man he recognized as Vern Milford on the head with a rock, knocking him out. He hauled the tall, skinny outlaw across his own saddle and walked the horse across the stream to where Carver and Gilpin waited.

CHAPTER 9

"Time for him to wake up," Pike said. "Toss some water on him."

Carver and Gilpin each filled his hat from the stream and tossed the water in Milford's face. Milford, who was sitting tied to a tree and gagged, shook his head and groaned in pain. He sputtered and tried to say something, but the gag prevented it.

Pike knelt in front of him. "We need to chat, Vern. To do so, I'll have to take the gag out of your mouth. However, let me tell you that if you try to yell a warning to the others, I will cut out your tongue and make you eat it. Is that clear?"

Milford searched Pike's face and decided he was serious. His eyes grew large, and he nodded.

Pike pulled the old piece of cloth from the outlaw's mouth. "What were you doin' out here?"

"Keepin' an eye out to see if anyone was

comin' into the canyon."

"Didn't do a very good job at it, did you?" Gilpin commented sarcastically.

Milford grimaced. "Didn't figure anyone'd know about this place, so I was just lollygaggin' about."

"The rest of you scum in the cabin?" Pike asked.

"Who you callin' . . . Um, yeah, all the boys're there. They're ready for trouble too."

"You're full of hog shit, Vern. If they thought trouble was on their doorstep, they would've sent out someone with more brains than you to do some scoutin', and whoever it was wouldn't have been lollygaggin' about. Who's the best rifle shot among the seven down there?"

"All of 'em could shoot the eye out of gnat at a hundred yards."

Pike slapped him so hard across the face that it sounded like a rifle shot and sent all the birds scattering. Milford's eyes crossed from the impact, then he shook his head to clear it.

"Vern, I am not of a mind to squat here and listen to you pour out claptrap. I want short, truthful answers, or you'll find yourself in a lot of pain with a lot of damage to your person. You understand that?"

"Yep," Milford muttered.

"Good. Now, who's the best rifle shot?"

"Be a tossup between Elroy Smith and Newt Grainer."

"What do they look like?"

"Regular guys, mostly. Medium height, weight. What surprises us all is how well Newt can handle a rifle considerin' one eye is cocked off to the side. You can tell Elroy from a distance 'cause his hair's kind of a strange color. Not red, not yellow, but something in between."

"Who's the best shooter close up?"

"Jethro's the best I ever saw. And me." When he saw Pike's dubious look, he said, "Give me back my Colt, and I'll prove it."

"Ain't likely I'll do so, but you'd come to a bad end if I did."

"Cocky bastard, ain't you?"

"With good reason. How well are you supplied in the cabin?"

"Damn good. We brought in plenty of food and some cattle. Plus, there's good huntin' and fishin' hereabouts. Weren't plannin' on stayin' here very long."

"Figurin' on leavin' soon, then?"

"Another couple days, maybe a week, accordin' to Jethro."

Pike looked up at Carver and Gilpin. Both nodded, indicating they knew how lucky they had been to get here when they did.

"There any windows on either side of the cabin?" Pike asked.

A sly look crossed Milford's face. "No. Nope. Just the ones at the front."

"Vern, what did I tell you about lying to me?"

Milford gulped. "Two windows on each side. No glass, just greased paper."

"Thank you, Vern." Pike placed his palms on his thighs and pushed to his feet. "Gag him," he ordered.

Carver moved before Milford had time to shout. He jammed the old cloth back into Milford's mouth and tied it in place with a bandanna.

"What now?" Gilpin asked.

"We wait 'til someone comes lookin' for Vern here and take him, then do the same with whoever comes lookin' for the two of 'em 'til we get all of 'em," Carver said.

"What makes you think they'll send anybody out lookin' for old Vern there?" Gilpin asked.

"Considerin' how stupid he seems to be, they'll likely figure he fell down and broke his neck or drowned in the stream," Carver tossed in.

"Or, hell, just got lost," Pike said.

The others chuckled.

"Besides," Gilpin added, "if he was to die,

there'd be one less man to share in the loot."

"Then we'll think of something else," Pike said, winking conspiratorially at his two companions. "But first we better eat," he added as the rain started.

They pulled on slickers and sat on rocks to gnaw on jerky. Gilpin pulled a pint bottle of redeye from a pocket in his slicker. When both other men shook their heads, he said, "Just one little sip to ward off the chill from the rain." He took one and passed the bottle to Pike, who did the same and passed it to Carver. He followed suit, then handed it back to Gilpin. The lawman corked it and placed it back into his pocket.

"You don't really think they'll send somebody out to look for Milford, do you?" Carver asked.

"Doubt it. At least not 'til tomorrow, but we'll keep an eye out for the rest of the day. If someone does come out, we'll try to grab him. I'd rather not get into a gunfight, though. Not while the others are holed up in there."

"So, have you come up with a plan, Brodie?"

"Of course," Pike said with a sarcastic grin. "A brilliant one, too."

"Well, are you gonna explain it, or do we have to guess?" Carver demanded.

"Might be too complicated for a couple of unsophisticated fellas like you." He laughed at the glares he received. "No, boys, it's really simple. Whether it'll work or not, well, that's open to question." He paused for a moment to take a sip of water, then continued, "Now that we know there're windows on the sides, we'll wait 'til dark and go on down there. Dex, you'll take the left side of the cabin. Sam, you'll take the right. When the action commences, tear through the greased paper and fire away."

"What about you?" Gilpin asked. "Plannin' to stay back here out of the line of fire?"

"No, Sam. I'll be goin' in through the front door."

"That's crazy."

"Have a better notion?"

"Well, no, but . . ."

"I should be able to get one or two of 'em in the first couple of seconds just by surprise. By then, I expect you two to start blastin' and take care of the rest of 'em."

Carver and Gilpin looked at each other and shrugged. "You think we're good enough to get the rest before they get you?" Carver asked.

"Don't know, but I sure as hell hope so. Besides, it's not like I'm aimin' to holster my Colts when I get inside."

"Sounds crazy enough to work, and it's time we brought this to an end," Carver said. "I'm in."

"Me, too," Gilpin agreed. He pulled out the bottle again. "One more sip to seal the pact."

They went through the ritual, but this time, instead of Carver giving the bottle back to Gilpin, he tossed it into the woods. "Don't need any more of that when we have important doin's ahead of us."

Gilpin looked a little aggrieved but he nodded.

"What do we do about him?" Carver asked, jerking a thumb at Milford.

"Leave him here and pick him up on our way back to Wolfsburg."

"Best make sure he's well secured," Gilpin said. "I'd hate to get shot in the back by him if he was to get free."

"He won't."

They talked little and about nothing important after that, each lost in his own thoughts. Before long, though, Pike said, "I reckon it's time to start movin'. With this rain, it's dark enough that we don't have to wait 'til night."

Pike rose and headed toward Milford, followed by his two companions. "Watch him," he said as he started to untie the outlaw. "If he tries anything, kick the stuffin' out of him. No shooting, though."

"Hell, nobody down there'll hear it anyway with the rain and thunder," Carver said.

"True. Best not to take chances, though. But if it's necessary, go ahead and plug him." He finished untying Milford. "Stand," he ordered. When the outlaw did, Pike tied his ankles tightly from behind and cut off the rope. He used that to lash his hands together, then threw the other end of the rope across a tree branch and tugged until Milford's hands were high above his head and his toes barely touching the ground. He tied the rope to another trunk. "Comfortable?" Pike asked, smiling grimly at Milford.

The outlaw's eyes bulged with anger, but all he could offer vocally were muffled grunts.

"Ready, boys?" Pike said. Both other men checked their weapons and nodded, then they all moved out on foot.

Because of the storm, they saw no need to try to sneak up on the cabin. They simply strode purposefully across the wide emptiness. Ten yards from the structure, they split, Carver going to the left, Gilpin to the right. Pike stopped and waited for a few moments for his companions to get into place.

Then he undid several buttons on his slicker, reached inside to rest his right hand on the butt of one Colt, took a deep breath, and marched forward.

He paused for a second at the door, then lifted the string holding the latch with his left hand. "Now, boys!" he bellowed as he shoved the door open and stepped inside, also drawing his other revolver. It required but a moment to take in the scene as seven sets of eyes turned his way.

The outlaws reacted more quickly than Pike had expected, but he did not hesitate. He fired once with each revolver and two outlaws went down, though he wasn't sure they were dead. Suddenly, bullets came from both sides as Carver and Gilpin tore open the greased paper and began shooting. The outlaws returned fire, and smoke filled the room, making it difficult to see.

Pike fired three more times, uncertain through the blue cloud whether he'd hit anyone. Then he was slammed back against the wall by a slug that tore into his upper chest, quickly followed by another only inches away. His back slid down the wall until he was sitting. He was a little surprised that there was no pain, though after a moment, he figured it was because he was near death. A blood-covered figure appeared out

of the cloud, pistol in hand. Without thinking, Pike fired, and the man went down.
Then he sank into the blackness.

CHAPTER 10

Brodie Pike strolled somewhat gingerly down the main street of Wolfsburg. It had been almost four months since the gun battle with the Harker gang, and he was still feeling some of the effects of his wounds, though he was mostly all right.

Somehow, Dex Carver and Sam Gilpin had managed to get him back to Wolfsburg alive. The doctor had pulled two .45 slugs out of him and done what he could to repair the internal damage, then left it up to Pike. Though he did not think the bounty hunter had much of a chance to live, Dr. Wills McKinney had hope. He figured that anyone who'd lost the amount of blood Pike had but was still alive after two days of travel had a strong constitution.

Indeed, that was the case, and within two weeks, Pike was up and about, though weaker than a newborn kitten. It was more than another month before he could hobble beyond a few steps, and another month or so before he began to get his strength back. Soon after that, he started practicing with his revolvers again, rapidly regaining his proficiency.

During his lengthy recovery, he learned what had happened after he was wounded.

Neither Carver nor Gilpin had been wounded. Mostly protected by the cabin's walls, thin as they were, and sowing confusion by firing from the sides, the outlaws were unable to fix on them as targets. The battle had lasted barely a minute. As soon as the last outlaw went down, the two lawmen swarmed into the cabin. While Gilpin checked on the outlaws, Carver checked on Pike.

"How is he?" Gilpin called as he kicked pistols out of the way. All of the outlaws were dead except one, and he would expire within an hour.

"Bad. Real bad. I don't think he'll make it another ten minutes, let alone how long it'd take us to get him to a sawbones."

"We're gonna try, though, ain't we?" Gilpin said more than asked.

"You bet, though I ain't sure how we'll get him anywhere."

"We could rig up a travois. Or somehow

make a cradle for him between two horses."

"I'll think about it. First, tear up a couple strips of a blanket so I can bind Brodie up. Maybe that'll stop the bleedin', or at least slow it down."

As the two men worked to bandage Pike, Gilpin asked, "What about these outlaws here?"

"What about 'em?"

"There's big rewards on all of 'em."

Carver paused in his work. "So?"

"Be a shame to let 'em rot here without us gettin' the rewards."

Carver glared at the younger man. "If I didn't need your help to get Brodie back to Wolfsburg, I'd shoot you here and now."

Gilpin tried to stare Carver down but couldn't quite manage it.

"Besides," Carver said, relenting a little, "we have Milford. We'll take him along, and he can be our witness that we took care of Harker and the rest of his boys."

Gilpin nodded, then mumbled, "Sorry. Money gets tight sometimes. And speakin' of money, there ought to be a hell of a lot of it here, considerin' how much these boys've stolen in the last month."

"So?"

"Be a shame to let it go to waste here, too."

Carver looked up at him and gave him a hateful stare. "You are some piece of work, Sam. Besides, that money ain't ours, so we'd have to get it back to those who lost it."

"Reckon you're right," Gilpin groused.

Carver just grunted in reply. Done binding Pike's wounds, he said, "See if you can find some long, thin logs lyin' around. If not, cut a couple."

Gilpin looked at him in question.

"A little different arrangement than your suggestion about hookin' horses together. Instead of side by side, we have one horse behind another, hooked together with the logs on the outside with a large gap in between. We put a stretcher in that gap."

"I can't quite picture it, but it makes sense." Gilpin paused, then said. "You do remember it's pitch-black out there? Can't see a damn thing more than a few feet away, if that."

"There're several lanterns around the room, and I think the rain's stopped, so there should be a little light."

Gilpin sighed but pushed up, grabbed a lantern, and quickly headed outside.

Carver made Pike as comfortable as he could under the circumstances. "Hold on, Brodie. We'll get you to a doc soon, and he'll fix you up," he said more to himself than to the unconscious Pike. He collected some rope and another lantern and went outside to help Gilpin.

"Looks like you got lucky," Carver said as Gilpin dragged up an eight-inch-round log and dropped it a few feet parallel to a similar one.

Gilpin swiped a hand across his forehead. "Damned glad I did, too. Those things are heavy, and if I'd had to cut 'em down, we'd be here a spell."

Carver nodded. "Go gather up what blankets you can from the cabin while I find a couple horses and saddle 'em."

Carver dropped the rope, then went to the rope corral and looked over the horses. He chose two that seemed sufficiently docile. He quickly saddled them and led them out and between the logs.

It took the two of them a few hours and a lot of work amid the intermittent rain that made it difficult to keep the lanterns lit to lash a log to each horse in tandem with a large gap between the animals. Then they rigged up a litter of blankets in that gap. As Carver was tying down the last of the blankets, Gilpin said, "I got an idea," and he trotted off. He was back in minutes with a pair of sturdy willow twigs, which he quickly tied into hoops attached to the litter. He tossed a piece of blanket over it and tied it down, creating a hood to keep the precipitation off Pike's face. By the time he finished, it was well into the night.

Shaking off his tiredness, Carver said, "Time to load up our patient." They handled Pike as gently as they could as they manhandled him into the litter. Despite the night's chill, both men were sweating.

Just before heading to the horses, Carver stopped. "I've heard Harker carried a special Colt, finely engraved along the barrel and with his initials in gold in the hickory grips. Let's find it. We can take it back as further proof that we got Harker's gang."

With a tired nod, Gilpin followed Carver into the cabin. The search didn't take long, and they soon had the revolver, which Carver stuck into his belt. As they prepared to leave, Gilpin suddenly said, "Food. There's something in the fire."

"Get it."

Outside again, Carver said, "I'm gonna let the rest of the horses go. They might follow. If they do, we'll have a few extra to use in case we need 'em. If not, they'll be free to do as they please."

Gilpin nodded, then said, "I think we

should burn the cabin, Dex."

"Sounds like a right good idea. Get to it while I free the other horses."

Gilpin went back inside, set his lantern down, found a container of coal oil, and spread it around. Just outside the door, he called, "You ready to leave, Dex?" With Carver's positive response, Gilpin tossed the lantern hard against the wall. The glass shattered, and flames burst out. The fire spread quickly despite the dampness of the outside walls.

Carver was already leading the horses carrying the litter back toward their old camp. Gilpin quickly caught up. Some of the freed horses followed along, but others trotted off.

Vern Milford was still hanging from the tree limb, alive but seemingly defeated. His eyes were wide, though, as he stared at the flames across the meadow.

Carver tied the makeshift ambulance to a tree. "Let's eat," he said.

Gilpin unwrapped the piece of buckskin in which he had wrapped a hunk of venison, still warm. The two quickly wolfed down the meat, and it served to revive them some.

After eating and taking a few swigs of water, the two men saddled their horses and Milford's, the latter after Carver tossed the outlaw's Winchester away. Carver untied the ropes and let Milford down. The outlaw's legs gave out on him, and he fell. With his hands still tied, he yanked the gag out of his mouth. "Water," he croaked.

Gilpin gave him a few sips from a canteen. "Food," Milford asked.

"You can afford to go a few days without food, even as skinny as you are. We don't have the time or the supplies to feed you. Now, get on your horse."

"Need help."

Carver pulled him to his feet. "Make one move against me, and I'll break a bone or two." He helped Milford onto his horse, and Gilpin tied his legs under the animal's belly.

Carver and Gilpin mounted, the former taking the lead and towing the horses carrying Pike. Milford came next, with Gilpin bringing up the rear. Several horses ended up following.

They moved as fast as they could without jouncing Pike too much in his precarious litter and stopped shortly after dawn for the first time. They threw together a small fire, cooked a couple rabbits Gilpin had shot, and made some coffee. They even let Milford eat a little. They allowed themselves a nap of two hours before hitting the trail again.

They pushed hard for the next couple of days, stopping only occasionally for a quick meal, an hour or two nap, and to change horses. Finally, exhausted, dirty, and frazzled, they pulled into Wolfsburg. First stop was Dr. Wills McKinney's office, where they left the wounded Brodie Pike. It surprised the physician considerably that he was still alive.

The next stop was the jail, where Gilpin reclaimed his job as Jefferson County sheriff and deposited Vern Milford in a cold, drafty cell. Then the two lawmen headed to a restaurant for a good meal and finally to Gilpin's house, where both collapsed and slept for most of twenty-four hours.

When they awoke, they made straight for the restaurant again, then checked on Pike. McKinney's prognosis wasn't good, but he held out some hope. "If you two didn't kill him by hauling him across all creation in that contraption you rigged up, he has a chance to come through this. A small one, I reckon, but a chance."

Carver and Gilpin left and went to get themselves cleaned up: shave, bath, haircut, even new duds. Then it was back to law business. The two became temporary co-sheriffs, an unusual situation, but one that the people accepted once the story of the battle with the Harker gang spread.

One of the first things they did was wire the nearest federal marshal, explaining things and requesting the reward. A few days later, Deputy U.S. Marshal Tim Walker showed up, talked to the two lawmen, and then questioned Milford, who tried to obfuscate for a while. Walker put up with it for only a short while before threatening the outlaw. Milford finally told the truth, and to seal the deal, Carver showed the marshal Harker's Colt.

"Looks like you boys got a heap of reward money coming," Walker said. "I'd like to buy that pistol from you, though. Give you a good price."

"Nope," Carver said.

"Well, I'll have the bank in Denver wire the reward money." He left town the next morning with Milford in chains.

More than a week later, Gilpin and Carver, who had been visiting daily, found Pike awake and coherent, though still weak and not quite ready to be up and about.

"Welcome back, Brodie," Carver said.

Pike grunted an acknowledgment, then asked, "How'd I get here?"

"All in good time, Brodie. You just rest easy and get back to your old self." Carver grinned. "But you won't have to worry about payin' the doc."

"I won't?" He wasn't much concerned about it anyway.

"Nope. Quite a bit of reward on those boys we took care of. A thousand bucks on Harker and five hundred each on the others."

Despite his lingering drowsiness, Pike was able to quickly total the amount. "Fifteen hundred each for the three of us."

"Yep. Even more. We got Harker's custom-made Colt. It's worth a heap — at least the deputy marshal who was here made a big offer — but we'd like you to have it."

"Yep," Gilpin added.

Pike glanced at Gilpin, who looked a little glum. "Sam doesn't seem so certain about it."

"He wants to sell it and split the money," Carver said.

"What about you?"

"I don't mean to say that I got something against money, but it ain't all that important to me. Sam thinks differently on the matter."

Pike thought a moment, then said, "How about I give you a hundred bucks for your share, Sam?"

"Might work," Gilpin said after a bit of

consideration. "But it'd have to be a bit more."

"Fifty, and no more."

"Hey, wait, you were supposed to offer more."

"You got thirty seconds to answer."

Gilpin fidgeted as Pike counted the time in his head. Then the bounty hunter said, "Twenty-five."

"Dammit, all right, you skunk."

"How about you, Dex? Something for your share? Maybe a hundred?" He grinned at the irate Gilpin.

"Nope. You deserve it."

Pike took the weapon and looked it over. "Damn fine piece of work, this Colt," he said, impressed. "Even without the engraving, it'd be a hell of a weapon."

As he was taking that stroll down the main street of Wolfsburg more than two months later, he decided to buy a newspaper from a young boy hawking them on the street. He soon returned to the room at a boarding house where he was now living and sat down to read. A headline near the bottom of the front page startled him.

"Two Rustlers Killed by Buckskin County Cattlemen's Association Detectives."

"Damn." He read that Hubert Dickson

and Garnet Blake, small ranchers, had been killed when they were caught taking several head of cattle from the ranch owned by Ulysses Hungerford, head of the cattlemen's group. Pike didn't believe the part about the two men rustling Hungerford's cattle.

Pike cursed again. Just as he had when he'd first helped Edgar Dunn, he knew he should not get involved now either. But now, as then, he knew he had to.

CHAPTER 11

Brodie Pike rode slowly and warily toward the McAllister house, which looked a bit more forlorn than it had more than three months ago. He was glad he was cautious as a shot rang out from the house, kicking up dust a few feet to Pike's left.

The shot was followed by a sharp voice: "Hold it right there, mister. Best turn 'round and move on. Next shot won't miss."

Pike stopped and called, "Charlie McAllister?"

"Who's askin'?"

"Brodie Pike."

"You alone?"

"Yep."

"Come ahead, then. Slow. Keep your hands where I can see 'em."

Pike did as he was told, stopping just in front of the cabin, not quite under the portico.

"Drop your guns."

"No."

"Do it, or I'll drop you where you sit." McAllister's voice was tense.

"I don't think you're that kind of man, Charlie."

"Shoot him, Charlie," another voice came from the house. Pike figured it was the quarrelsome Clay Dunn.

There were some moments of silence before McAllister said, "All right, come on in."

Pike was not surprised that he faced several guns when he entered the room. "Hell of a welcome," he said with a small smile.

"You're lucky I just don't kill you here and now," Dunn said.

Pike looked at McAllister. "He hasn't changed any, has he?"

"Nope. But he has some reason now to be suspicious of any gunman who shows up here."

"Reckon he does," Pike said with a nod, "if what I read in the newspaper is true."

"It is." McAllister nodded at the table. "Well, not the part about rustlin', of course. Have a seat, Mr. Pike." When the bounty hunter had done so, McAllister uncocked his Winchester and leaned it against the wall. He nodded at the other men to holster their pistols, then he sat across from Pike.

Viv McAllister and Marcy McAllister, the former Charlie's wife and the latter his sixteen-year-old daughter, and Cora Dunn came out of a back room and poured coffee for the two men.

"So, why are you here, Mr. Pike?" McAllister asked.

"Came to see if I can give you some help."

"Kind of late, ain't it?" Dunn snapped. "What the hell've you been doin' the last three, four months? Drinkin' and whorin'?"

The women gasped.

"I wish I had been. But I've been recuperating."

"From what? The clap?"

The women gasped again in shock, and Cora Dunn, Clay's sister-in-law, said, "Watch your mouth, Clay Dunn. There's no call for such language."

Dunn started to retort but snapped his mouth shut, realizing it would be folly to continue.

Pike was trying hard to keep his fast-rising anger under control and mostly managed, though there was a bit of it in his voice when he said, "Recuperating from a couple of bullets to the chest."

"You lyin' . . ."

McAllister overrode his impetuous

128

brother-in-law. "What happened?"

"Had a gunfight with the Harker gang."

"I take it they left you for dead and took off?" McAllister asked.

"Nope. Seven of 'em died in a cabin in a canyon. The other one was brought to Wolfsburg, and then carted off by a U.S. deputy marshal."

"How?" McAllister asked, confused and suspicious.

"Had help. Couple of lawmen. They managed to drag me back to Wolfsburg — more than two hard-ridin' days for 'em — to get me to a doc. Five days ago, I saw a newspaper in Wolfsburg and headed here right away."

"I don't believe a word of it," Dunn said.

It took a great effort this time for Pike to tamp down the rage that boiled inside him. "I don't much give a good god — hoot what you think, boy," he snapped. Then through tight lips, he said, "If you ladies would be so kind as to turn away for a moment." When they did, Pike undid several buttons on his shirt and pulled it open, exposing the still-raw wounds. After a few moments, he buttoned his shirt. "All right, ladies, you can turn around again." He turned hard eyes on Dunn. "I've given you a lot of leeway in the few times we've met, boy, but if you question me or my integrity again, I'll kill you whether Charlie or any of the others try to stop me. You understand that, boy?"

Dunn couldn't stare back. He dropped his eyes. "Yes, sir," he mumbled.

"Speak up, Clay," McAllister snapped.

"I understand."

"I'm thankful that you've come to offer your help, Mr. Pike," McAllister said. "But I'm afraid it might be too late. A lot's gone on in the months you've been away. You know, of course, about Hubert and Garnet. They also got Artie Mathews last week."

"I'm not surprised."

"We are. Not so much that they killed some of us, but that they haven't come at us full force. We thought maybe they were reconsiderin' your suggestions, but we don't know that for certain. Maybe they just wanted us to think things had calmed down, let us relax a little, and then pounce. Which was what we did and they did."

"Sounds like something they'd do, maybe. But I think they got something else in mind."

"What's that?"

"I've come across men like Hungerford before. They're not only greedy, they're evil. I reckon it was a couple weeks between the first two killin's?"

"A little more, maybe a month. A little longer before they got Artie."

"Anything else?"

"Few shots fired at the Morgan place, and someone tried to burn down the Dickson barn. They managed to save that, though."

Pike nodded. "That'd be just how a man like Hungerford would act."

"How so?"

"Like I said, men like Hungerford are evil. He's got enough guns to attack all at once and drive you off, but for him, there's more pleasure in toyin' with you and torturin' you. Kill one of you now and again, time enough apart that you'll just be startin' to settle down, thinkin' things'll get better, then another one to make you jumpy again. Random shots at various places of yours, a fire here and there. Maybe even kill a few cattle from time to time. He'll likely thump some of your people if they go into Graystone, or at least harass 'em like they did Ed."

Cora Dunn sucked in a deep breath of renewed grief.

"Bastards!" Felder said, not caring if the language upset the women. None of them said anything.

"So, what can you do?" McAllister asked.

"The situation hasn't changed much. A killin' now and again to keep us jumpy and scared. Hungerford's got more gunmen than when you were last here, and you're by yourself."

"There are problems for sure," Pike said dryly. "Be honest, I don't know if there's much of anything I can do. But I aim to do whatever I can."

"Ain't you afraid of getting' shot again?" asked Matt McAllister, Charlie's oldest son.

"Well, I ain't plannin' on getting' shot again. 'Course, I didn't plan on gettin' shot by Harker's boys either." There were a few nervous chuckles around the room. "But it doesn't pay to think about such things. It does pay to plan things as best you can and don't go rushin' into 'em. But things don't always work out the way you plan."

"Well, I reckon that since you just got here, you don't have a plan yet," Charlie McAllister said.

"True. But I did some thinkin' on the trail. I figure I best prowl around, see what's what. Maybe I can come up with some way to better our odds a little at a time. Meanwhile, keep a close eye out. Seein' the greetin' I received, I figure you're bein' cautious."

"Yep. We did let our guard down some,

but when our people got killed, we tightened up again. The McAllisters and Dunns have mostly forted up here. A couple of the other families have done the same. When we go out to tend the cattle, we have a few hands — those who stayed with us — keepin' a watch out. A few of the folks just took off, drivin' some of their cattle off. And we always leave at least one of the men here, armed, of course."

"Wise. Seems you're doing the right things. I can't guarantee I can end all your troubles with the cattlemen, but I'll do what I can."

"We're much obliged."

"And how much do we have to pay you for this maybe, maybe no protection?" Dunn asked.

With a bland expression, Pike said, "A thousand dollars for every one of Hungerford's men I dispose of."

Dunn's eyes bugged in outrage and he looked as if he wanted to spew out an angry retort, but he couldn't manage speech.

McAllister, too, was shocked, but only for a moment. Then he grinned. "Had me goin' there for a moment, Mr. Pike."

Pike grinned back.

"You mean he was joshin'?" Dunn finally managed.

"Of course he was, you fool."

"It won't cost you anything, Clay. I figure I owe you folks something, seein' as I more or less started it when I helped Ed. I might as well try to finish it."

McAllister nodded. "Well, you're welcome to stay here, though you'll have to bunk in the barn."

"That'll do."

"You hungry?"

"Yep."

"Viv, some food for our guest, please."

Pike breakfasted on some of last night's supper he had brought to the barn. It was sparse and quickly disposed of. Then he saddled up and rode out. The people in the house were just stirring.

As he supped the night before, Charlie McAllister had provided him with as much detail as he could about Hungerford's ranch and the area. Using that information, Pike headed toward the ranch a dozen or so miles mostly east of McAllister's place, on the other side of the small tree-peppered mountain.

Pike stopped amid the oaks and pines on a hill overlooking the place. It was a large house made of good planed wood, painted a rich, chocolate brown with gold-colored shutters and trim. A porch curved around at least the front and both sides; Pike couldn't see if it continued across the back. To the right was the corral and stable, as well as a barn and a carriage house. About a dozen horses stood in the corral, and Pike figured there was possibly the same number inside the stable. To the left was the bunkhouse for fifteen or so men, twenty if they lived close together. Pike estimated there were ten to twelve "detectives." Beyond the house, Pike could see a vast meadow with cattle grazing. There was another bunkhouse out there, this one for the men handling the cattle, Pike figured. The one near the house was for the hired guns, he assumed.

He spent the next two days wandering the area, observing, learning, and trying to formulate a plan to free the McAllisters and Dunns and their friends and neighbors, the Felders, the Blakes, the Dicksons, the Morgans, and the Mathews clans of the cattlemen's oppression. He would sup with the family, and as he did the first night, take a little food with him for the morning. He was on the trail as dawn was breaking.

After those two days, he was close to concluding that there really was little he could do, but he was determined not to give up. He was made more determined when

Hungerford's men burned the barn at the Blake place. Two horses and a milk cow died in the conflagration. McAllister and the others were all on edge again.

The next day, Pike stopped on the small hill about a quarter-mile from Hungerford's ranch house, chewing on a biscuit and watching. A man came out of the lodging, mounted a horse that had been tied out front, and started moving toward the hill some distance to Pike's left, toward the homes of McAlister and the others.

Pike sat for a few moments, then curled his lips in a grim smile. He mounted his horse, rode back into the trees, and turned in the direction he had seen the rider go. It was only a few minutes before he caught sight of the man through the pines. He pulled his Winchester out of the saddle scabbard and rode quietly up behind him, then said, "Hey, mister."

The man, startled, turned in his saddle, and Pike smashed him across the face with the barrel of the rifle. The man reeled in the saddle, his face bloody and his eyes glazed.

Pike slid the Winchester away, reached over, grabbed the gunman's pistol, and tossed it away. Then he took the reins of the man's horse and led it across the hill to a rocky slope nearby.

He dismounted and yanked the man off his horse. The outlaw was groggy but coming around some. "Who the hell are you?" he demanded, voice slurred.

"Your executioner. I don't like it when two-bit scum like you go around killin' decent, innocent folks. It's time for you to pay for it."

"I didn't kill anybody 'round here."

"Doesn't matter. If it wasn't you, it was one of your fellow pukes. You're all the same."

The outlaw started to rise, but Pike kicked him in the chin, knocking him back down. Without another word, Pike pulled his knife and stabbed the outlaw in the heart. He wiped the blade off on the man's shirt, then dragged the body to a small cave in the hillside and shoved it in. He got the man's saddle and the rest of the tack and dumped it in after the carcass, then threw some dirt and rocks into the cave and rolled a few boulders over the opening. The hole wasn't covered, but unless someone was looking, the body would not be found.

He wiped some sweat off his brow, then slapped the outlaw's horse's rump hard, sending it racing down the hill. With a last look at the makeshift grave, he muttered,

"It ain't much, but it's one less son of a bitch to worry about." He rode off.

CHAPTER 12

Pike was less lucky the next day; he didn't see any of Hungerford's gunmen other than at a distance across a meadow. In annoyance, he went back to the McAllisters' place.

"Glad you stopped by," Charlie McAllister said as they sat at the table in the house. Felder and his brother Jules, Clay Dunn, and Matt McAllister took seats too.

"What's up?" Pike nodded thanks as Viv put some coffee before him.

"We're goin' into Graystone tomorrow. Need you to stay here and watch over things."

"Might be best if I rode along, and you leave some of the others here."

"Too dangerous. The 'detectives,' " he spat the word, "see us leavin', and they might just come against the house. With you here, the women'll have a chance."

"Good thinkin'. But if I'm ridin' with you, I'll likely see anyone watchin', and I'll disabuse them of the notion of goin' against the house."

"How're you gonna do that, ridin' with us? They could be hidin' and watchin'."

"Won't be ridin' with you exactly." At McAllister's questioning look, he continued, "I'll be ridin' near you, scoutin', keeping an eye out for any of Hungerford's gunmen."

"What do you think, Con?" McAllister asked his cousin.

Connor Felder thought for a few moments, then shrugged. "Dangerous either way, Charlie. He goes with you, Hungerford's scum could attack the house. He stays here, they could attack you with the wagon. You likely wouldn't have a chance on your own. You might if he's along."

"Hadn't thought of that." It was McAllister's turn to cogitate. Then he nodded. "Be glad to have you along, Brodie."

Pike bobbed his head. "I'll be up and out before dawn, so just leave when you plan to. If things look okay, I'll join you somewhere on the road." He paused. "If you hear shootin', head here fast if you're still close, or race for Graystone if you're closer to there. That happens, get to cover wherever you can. If I'm able, I'll join you."

"What do you mean, 'if you're able?' " Felder asked.

"Even as good as I am, I can't take on too many all at once. Learned that in the canyon in Jefferson County not so long ago."

"Ah, yeah," Felder mumbled, feeling like a fool.

"Thought I saw something wrong with one of the mule's shoes, Charlie," Pike said. Baffled, McAllister looked at Pike. "Reckon you ought to check it out."

McAllister thought to argue but stopped when he saw the look in Pike's eye. "Reckon I should if we're leavin' first thing in the mornin'."

When he and Pike walked outside, McAllister asked, "What's this about, Brodie? There's nothing wrong with those mules."

"I know. Just wanted to see what you were thinkin' about Clay."

"What do you mean?"

"Take him with you or leave him here?"

"Thought of takin' him. He might be a hothead sometimes, but he's a hard worker and strong."

"I thought you might be thinkin' that. I'm thinkin', though, that's a bad idea."

"Why?"

"Like you said, he's a hothead. Unless Hungerford's men attack the house, he should be okay. If they do, he could do something stupid. But I'm pretty certain

Hungerford's men won't do that. I think Hungerford's enjoyin' the terror he's creatin'. Everyone should be all right if they don't wander too far from the house, so it's better to leave him here. If you take him to town, him being the fool he is, he could do something stupid. That would likely be a serious and deadly business."

"Damned if we do, damned if we don't," McAllister said with a wry grin.

"Well, one damned is a little less damned than the other damned."

McAllister laughed. "Hell of a way to put it, but I reckon you're right. And you're right about Clay. I'll take Connor and Viv. We need a woman along to get some of the goods."

Pike nodded. "See you tomorrow sometime."

"Yeah. And thanks, Brodie, for everything."

"Ain't done much yet, Charlie."

"What you've done is a lot better'n nothin'."

Pike pulled out before daybreak, just as McAllister was heading to the barn to hitch the mules to the wagon. The bounty hunter was chewing on a biscuit saved from the day before. It wasn't much, but he didn't want to waste time with breakfast at the house before getting on his way. He rode toward Hungerford's ranch, taking his time, keeping a watch out as best he could in the dark. Just after dawn, he was at his perch on the hill above the ranch. Men soon drifted out of the bunkhouse, heading for the three-seater outhouse, then into the main house for breakfast, Pike figured. And to get orders for the day, he thought sourly.

Before long, the men wandered out and began saddling their horses. Three rode off in the general direction of the McAllister place, and four others up the road over the hill a quarter mile to Pike's right. They could be heading anywhere, including to town, which meant using the road McAllister would be on.

Pike sat there, considering what to do. The wagon was vulnerable out in the open with just two men and a woman. The house was more protected, with several men there to guard it, as long as Clay Dunn didn't do anything too rash. He didn't think Hungerford's men would actually go against them, not when he could have his men keep the small-time ranchers cowering behind thick wood walls.

Pike turned and headed toward the road to Graystone. He stayed among the trees, wary but pretty certain he would not run into the four gunmen. He crested another ridge and turned toward the McAllisters', paralleling the road amid the trees. Within five minutes, he saw the wagon. With a nod, he swung around and picked up the pace a little. Before long, he slowed when he spotted the four men he had seen leave the ranch on the road. They were plodding slowly along, in no hurry to get anywhere, it seemed. Once again, he turned and headed back the way he had come.

He came out of the trees a little ahead of the wagon, pleased that Felder reached for his rifle as soon as he saw a rider. He put it back down when he recognized Pike. McAllister halted the conveyance alongside the bounty hunter. "News?" He asked.

"A few of Hungerford's men are headed toward your place, but I get the feeling they weren't going to cause trouble unless Clay pushes it. They might not even show themselves. Just keep an eye on the place, though they might just put a round or two down toward the house just to keep everyone on edge."

"Well, that's good, I guess. Since you're here, I figure the road is clear?"

"Nope. But no real danger either. I want you to take a break. Pull off the road into

144

the woods a little just down the road a piece. Four of Hungerford's men are headed to town, movin' at a snail's pace. I don't want you catchin' up to 'em."

"Sounds like a right fine idea," McAllister said with a rueful smile.

"Should we wait long enough to have a bite and maybe make some coffee?" Viv McAllister asked.

"I believe that'd be a good idea, ma'am."

"We have some eggs we plan to sell in town. We could fry up a few for you, seein' as how you skipped out on breakfast, Brodie."

"I believe that's an even better idea, ma'am," Pike said with a grin. Looking at McAllister, he said, "There's a good spot about half a mile on where you can pull into the trees. I'm gonna go check on our 'friends' up ahead, then hustle on back for some food."

"See you soon, Brodie," McAllister said.

Pike nodded and headed up the road. If the gunmen had stopped and were waiting for him, so be it. He would face it and be done with several more of Hungerford's gun hands, he thought cockily.

He slowed abruptly when he spotted them ahead and darted into the woods, moving farther into the trees as he rode forward.

He got ahead of them and waited for a bit. They were still plodding along, smoking and joking, showing no signs that they were wary of or expecting to see anything out of the ordinary.

Satisfied, Pike rode back to McAllister's wagon, taking a little time to cross the road back and forth several times, riding deeper into the trees to see if anyone else was about. He could smell the coffee and the pine smoke, and he worried for a minute since anyone within a mile of the windward side of the forest probably could smell it. But he shrugged it off. The McAllister place was a few miles back, and Hungerford's ranch was a number of miles upwind and over a few hills. He could see no trouble in it.

He stopped and dismounted and loosened the horse's cinch. "Coffee smells good, ma'am."

She smiled shyly, then asked, "You want those eggs now?"

"If it ain't too much trouble."

"None a'tall."

As Pike sat and took the mug of coffee Viv proffered, McAllister asked, "Any trouble?"

"Nope. Those boys are moseyin' on like they got all year to get to town. No one else about either. I figure if you wait another thirty minutes or so and then push on, takin' your time, you'll be all right. I'll still be out ridin' ahead, keepin' an eye on things."

"Obliged."

Pike just nodded and sipped his coffee, then ate the eggs Viv had made. They were tasty though not very filling, but Pike said nothing. He did not want to hurt the woman's feelings. He even refused a second helping.

It was not long before Pike tightened his cinch. He mounted and said to McAllister, "I'll likely follow those boys all the way to Graystone, but I don't think it's smart to show my face in town, so you might not see me again 'til you're on your way back here. Unless you're plannin' on spendin' the night in town?"

"Nope," McAllister said. "The less time we spend there, the better."

"Good thinkin'." Pike rode off.

The four gunmen were still making no haste toward Graystone, though they never slowed or deviated. They arrived shortly after noon.

Sticking to the woods, he rode slowly through the trees along the stream on the south side of town. It ran about twenty yards from the back of several cribs behind the saloon and farther from some of the town's businesses. He stopped there. On his left was Franklin's general store. Next to it on the right, across a wide, trash-strewn alley, was a restaurant. Despite a growling stomach, he could not risk going inside, so he stayed among the trees along the creek, watching.

Soon after, between the buildings, he saw McAllister's wagon moving up the main street. It stopped in front of Franklin's, the back end of it just visible between the wall of the store and the billiard parlor next door to Pike's left.

It took some time, and Pike was beginning to get itchy before he saw Connor Felder and Charlie McAllister start to load the wagon. They worked quickly and were soon finishing.

"Damn," Pike suddenly spat. He jumped on his horse and galloped down the alley before stopping at the end. Then he slid out of the saddle and charged forward, drawing his knife instead of his pistol.

CHAPTER 13

Pike grabbed the hair of one of Hungerford's men, jerked his head back, and slid the knife blade across the man's throat. The "detective" sputtered as blood gushed from his suddenly gaping throat.

Pike pushed the gun hand away and shouted to McAllister, who was standing there with his rifle, trying to decide what to do about the other gunmen who had appeared, "Go, Charlie! Move!"

"What about . . ."

"Just get out of here. Anybody shows any interest in you, just tell him you saw violence break out and you made dust!" As he talked, he had slid the bloody knife back into its sheath and pulled a Colt.

Two of the other gunmen he had followed into Graystone were moving on the street side of the wagon; the other was coming around the mules. Pike swung toward him first. In the split second after Viv McAllister had climbed aboard the wagon next to her husband, Pike fired and dropped the one near the team.

Felder jumped into the back of the wagon with the supplies, and McAllister slapped the reins hard. "C'mon, mules, move!"

The vehicle started slowly but picked up a little speed as McAllister swung the animals about in a U-turn.

With the wagon moving out of the way, the other two gunmen were exposed, though not unprepared. Both fired, but Pike was already moving. He dived behind a wood trough as a bullet clipped the side of his hat and another thudded into the wall of the store Pike had been behind a moment before. He laid there for a moment, replacing the spent shell and adding a sixth cartridge. The two fired at the trough, doing no harm since the water slowed the slugs down.

Pike gingerly spun and then popped up on the side of the trough where the others would expect his feet to be. Both gunmen jerked their pistols toward Pike, but they were a moment too late. Pike shot both in the chest twice, then he ran and jumped on his horse. He spun the animal around and raced down the alley and across the short, weedy stretch of land, then splashed across the stream and dashed into the woods.

He angled southwest, away from the direction McAllister was heading, and pushed the horse hard up the tree-covered hill but eased up when they went down the other side. The animal moved warily though steadily, its hooves slipping now and again on the grass and dirt.

Finally on the flat and covered by various pines, Pike kicked the horse into a gallop. He kept up the pace for several miles until the land began to rise sharply. Slowing some, he turned south, moving even farther from McAllister's place. He kept off the slope, instead riding along the bottom for another couple of miles. Then he turned the horse onto the incline, stopping only when he reached the top.

He dismounted and unsaddled the horse, then let it drink from a small pool formed by a little bubbling spring. As the adrenaline slowed, Pike's hunger reasserted itself, and he cursed himself for skipping the second helping of eggs when McAllister and the others had stopped. Finally, he sighed. There was nothing to do about missing the meal. He rummaged in his saddlebags and came up with two strips of jerky. It would have to suffice.

He gently tugged to horse away from the

small waterhole and off a little to let it graze, then filled his canteen and sat. Alternately gnawing on the jerky and sipping the almost-fresh water, he contemplated the future, both the near and slightly more distant. Killing Hungerford's four gunmen had been unfortunate though necessary, and it was certain to lead to more trouble, though it did lessen the odds considerably.

A deer cautiously edged through the trees not more than twenty feet away, and Pike sat without moving. The thought of fresh venison made Pike's mouth water, but he could not risk the gunshot. He had no idea if a posse from Graystone was on his trail, but if one were, the sound would draw it to him. He tossed a rock at the deer, and it skittered away. "Don't come back, either," he mumbled. "Or I'll chance it." He smiled ruefully.

Dusk was rapidly falling, and Pike decided he would spend the night here. He wasn't sure where he was, and trying to find his way in this heavily forested area in the dark would be folly.

Pike finished his sparse meal, then stretched out on his bedroll and, using his saddle as a pillow, drifted off to sleep.

Dawn came slowly for him. It was a gray, windy opening of the morning, souring his day right from the start. Having no food did not improve his mood any. He stretched, relieved himself, refilled his canteen, and then spent some minutes scanning his back trail. There appeared to be no one following him. He had that in his favor at least. He finally saddled the horse, donned his oilcloth slicker against the light rain that had begun, and headed west. Soon, though, he turned northeast, in the direction of Graystone, though well to the west of it. Around midday, he turned southeast, passing the town but giving it a wide berth. Far to the east of Graystone, he swung northwest, and in a few hours, he was sitting atop the hill overlooking Hungerford's place.

Nothing seemed out of the ordinary, and Pike wondered what was going on. He was a little surprised that the cattleman had not sent out men to look for him or for the four men who had gone to Graystone. It was likely, though, that he didn't know about the four men being dead unless someone had ridden out from town to tell him. That didn't seem likely from where Pike sat. Still, he wondered what Hungerford would do when he did learn about it. He might send his boys on a full-out assault on the small ranchers, but he might also wait until he could hire more gunmen. That would be both good and bad: good because it would give him and the others more time to prepare, bad because they would be facing more guns and an angry Hungerford, who might just send his army after the McAllisters and their friends. If the former was the case, maybe a solution would present itself. If the latter, the future for him and the others would be dim and short.

With daylight, such as it was, fading fast and heavier rain pelting him, Pike headed toward the McAllister place.

When he rode into the barn, Abe McAllister, Charlie's youngest son at about eleven, who was milking the two dairy cows the family kept, jumped up, startled. The cows shifted nervously at his sudden movement.

"Sorry, Abe," Pike said as he dismounted and slapped the water off his hat.

"That's all right, Mr. Pike," the boy said, composure returning. "Want me to tell the folks you're back?"

"Finish up your chore, Abe. That's more important. Then you can do so. I've got to tend my horse first anyway."

"Yes, sir."

The boy was done soon after and left. He returned as Pike was finishing taking care of his mount.

"Pa says he'd like to talk to you, Mr. Pike, and Mom wants to know if you're hungry."

"Tell your ma I'm as hungry as a newly woke grizzly bear. And I want to talk to Charlie, too, so let's go before the grumblin' in my stomach scares all the animals."

Chuckling, the boy ran ahead through the undiminished rainfall.

Pike entered the house, shook the water off his slicker and hat, and hung them on a peg next to the door. He paid the people scattered around no heed as his hungry eyes fixated on the beefsteak overlapping a plate that awaited him. He sat and started bolting down the meat, enjoying the first bite more than any other he had ever had, he thought. After several mouthfuls of the meat and some of the accompanying yams, he said, "Sorry to ignore you folks, but I was a mite hungry."

"A mite," McAllister said with a chortle. "The way you're wolfin' down that steak looks like you ain't eaten in a week."

"Feels like it." He finally slowed, chewing more sedately, then grabbed a biscuit and slathered butter on it. Moments later, it had disappeared down his throat.

"More?" Viv McAllister asked.

"If it wouldn't be any trouble."

She smiled. "I thought you might want

155

another, so I cooked it up. It's been kept warm for you. More yams, too?"

"Yes'm." He was more restrained in his eating now. As he chewed, he looked at McAllister and asked, "You kill one of your beeves?"

McAllister controlled himself so he would not retort and said evenly, "Comes from a stray we found."

Pike grinned. "The cow that strays pays."

Everyone breathed a sigh of relief.

Finished, Viv filled his coffee cup again, then she and the other women went into another room.

"You have any trouble on the way back, Charlie?" Pike asked.

"Nope. Most of the folks in Graystone don't like Hungerford — well, his gunmen, anyway — any more than we do, so they ain't likely to chase after us when a bunch of those damned gunmen come to a bad end. Marshal Haney might've tried to raise a posse, though if he did, which I doubt, he likely didn't get many volunteers. How about you?"

"Reckon not. I put some ground between me and the town pretty quick. Didn't see any sign all day that anyone was followin' me. If what you say about the townsfolks' feelin's toward Hungerford, it probably kept a posse from followin' me, too."

"Well, now that you killed four of his men, Hungerford's likely to be mighty upset, which could cause us a heap of trouble," Clay Dunn said.

"Thought that's what you wanted," Pike snapped, annoyed. "Not that I did it for the hell of it or because you suggested I do so."

"Well, I didn't mean it that way."

"You sure as hell did, Clay," McAllister said sharply. "Now, me and Brodie have both told you more than once to stop makin' foolish comments. Don't open your mouth again unless you have something helpful to say." He turned back to Pike. "Any idea of what Hungerford might be plannin'? He can't be happy about losin' four men, especially in front of the people in Graystone."

"Can't say. He might not even know yet. Unless some of his gunmen miss their pals, it might be a while 'til he finds out. Though again, if what you said about the townsfolks' feelings toward him is true, I don't know there's many who'd want to bother tellin' him."

He swallowed some more steak, then said, "I rode past his place before headin' here. There didn't seem to be much activity." He explained his thoughts on the possibilities.

"Well, I reckon he's short four more men, even if he doesn't know they're dead. When he learns about it, I'd expect he'll be hirin' new ones. That your thinkin', Brodie?"

"Reckon so."

"So, what do we do?"

"I can't tell you that." He held up his hand to stem any protests. "Like before, I can only give my opinion of the situation."

"So, opine."

"Well, if he is plannin' to hire more gunmen once he hears about those five, it'll take a while for them to get here. Meantime, there are a few things we can do. Since you're already forted up, some of the outlying houses are vulnerable, but not much can be done about that. I suggest you get all your stock as close to the two places as you can, or if you know of someplace that ain't easy to find, drive 'em there and leave one or two men to watch over 'em. I think you need to stockpile supplies: food, water, wood, and as many guns and as much ammunition as you can. We'll teach everyone, includin' the women and the young'uns maybe twelve and older, to use the firearms. Also, add shutters to all the windows."

"The last won't stop them fellas from burnin' the place down. Only give 'em more fuel," Connor Felder said.

"That's true, but like I said a while ago, I think the Cattlemen's Association, or at least some of the members, will be reluctant to come against us in a full-out assault. Killin' a bunch of women and kids, especially by burnin' 'em, won't sit well with many officials, even if they are in the association's pocket."

"I hope you're right," McAllister said.

"Me, too," Pike agreed. "I'd also have someone on the roof at all times."

"Even at night?" Dunn asked.

"Yep. I reckon Hungerford's men, if they come straight at us, won't be worried about being seen, so if you spot their movement in the dark, it'll give us time to get ready. And if you send the herds off, make sure the fellas you send with 'em pay attention at all times."

"You'll stick with us, Brodie?" Felder asked.

"Yep. I'll likely be out there most of the time, though, keeping an eye out so I can give the rest of you some warning if he sends his men against us."

"We got us a lot of thinkin' to do on all this, Brodie," McAllister said.

Pike nodded, then rose. "I'll be in the barn. Think I'll stop in for breakfast before

I ride out scoutin'," he said with a small smile.

CHAPTER 14

Pike reached for his revolver at the soft knock on the barn door. "Come ahead."

The door opened slowly, and Pike cocked the pistol. Marcy McAllister, Charlie's sixteen-year-old daughter, shyly entered. She started when she saw the firearm pointed in her direction.

Pike smiled and uncocked the six-gun and returned it to its holster. "Sorry, ma'am. A man like me never knows who's gonna come visitin' in the night."

Marcy blushed.

"What brings you here in the dark, young lady?"

"Thought you might like some of my peach pie," she said, holding out a plate with one hand.

"No, ma'am." At her crushed look, he grinned widely. "That is, not if you ain't got coffee or even milk to go with it."

Relief crossed her face, and she grinned.

Her other arm came out from behind her back, holding a glass of milk.

"Well, ain't you something now," he said, beckoning her to come closer. She did and handed him the pie and milk. "Thank you, Marcy."

"Mind if I sit while you eat your pie?" the girl asked.

Pike looked askance at her. "Your folks know you're out here?"

She hesitated for a moment. "Yep. Mama wanted me to bring this to you."

Raising an eyebrow at her, Pike said, "Lyin' ain't becoming to such a pretty girl."

Marcy flushed a deeper pink this time. "I . . ."

"I'm obliged for the pie and the milk, but you best get on back to the house before your ma catches you out here and takes a switch to both of us." But he grinned.

As she disappeared, Pike stared at the barn door for some minutes. Marcy was a fine-looking young woman with a pretty face, long, curly russet hair, and a well-formed figure. But she was only sixteen. That was plenty old enough to marry. Many girls of fifteen or sixteen were married, but he was more than ten years her senior. Unions of such age differences were also common, but the idea of it left him a bit

162

uncomfortable. Taking advantage of her without the benefit of marriage did not enter his mind. Such a thing simply was not done by a decent fellow, and despite his profession, he considered himself to be a decent man. He sighed and turned in and was quickly asleep.

He hurried through breakfast at the house in the morning and hit the trail, roving the area, but he saw nothing untoward. He reported that as he supped with McAllister's family, knowing he was being surreptitiously stared at by Marcy throughout the meal.

The young woman visited him again that night, bearing pie and milk. They chatted, Marcy hinting at a growing attraction to him, he being noncommittal.

The next two days and evenings were the same, and it began to bother Pike. He did not want to give Marcy any indication that he was interested in marrying her. At the same time, he did not want to insult or hurt her.

So after supper, he rode out again, not saying anything. Two days ago, McAllister had had some of his friends drive all their cattle to a secluded box canyon a few miles west and higher in the mountains, and Pike wanted to see it.

He rode through the narrow neck of the canyon and went unchallenged even as he walked his horse slowly amid the small herd of softly lowing cattle. He caught the glint of embers from a fire that had burned low. He turned that way, stopped when he was ten yards away, and dismounted. Pike walked up to where a young man was sleeping and knelt, pulling his pistol as he did. He cocked the weapon.

The sound, not loud but distinctive, woke the young man, and his eyes widened in fear. Then he recognized Pike in the thin light of the half-moon. "You alone?" Pike asked.

"Arch is here somewhere."

"Anyone else?"

"No."

"Arch ain't keepin' watch. Where is he?"

"He was supposed to be watchin' out." He relaxed a little when Pike uncocked his revolver and dropped it back into its holster.

"Where?"

"All 'round. He was supposed to wake me later to take over."

"Well, if he was on watch, he ain't very alert. Call him."

"Arch!" Vin Mathews shouted. He pushed himself up until he was sitting. "Arch!"

"What'n hell you want, Vin?" a groggy

voice came floating to them from not too far away.

"Best get your hide over here, Arch!"

"Go to hell, Vin. I'm tired."

"If I have to come get you, young fella," Pike said in a normal voice but one that carried, "you'll regret it."

"Yes, sir," a worried voice said from the darkness. "On my way."

Moments later, Arch Blake was standing at the dying fire alongside Pike and Vin Mathews. The two young men stood with their heads hanging in embarrassment.

"Maybe your elders didn't explain things to you properly, but one of you was supposed to be on watch all the time," Pike said in a harsh voice.

"But I . . ."

"Shut your trap, Arch," Mathews said. "Mr. Pike's right, and you sure as the devil know it."

"If I was one of Hungerford's hired guns, you boys'd both be dead and all your families' cattle gone. You two understand how serious this duty you've been given is?"

"Didn't," Mathews mumbled.

"Do you now?"

"Yes, sir," the young men answered in unison.

"All right, then. Build up the fire a bit,

165

have a bite and maybe some coffee, then decide which one of you, Arch," he added with a grin, "takes first watch."

"You'll share some coffee with us, Mr. Pike?" Blake asked.

"Hopin' to keep from startin' your duties, Arch?" He laughed at the shocked look on Blake's face. "I would've done the same. Sure, I'll take some Arbuckle's with you."

As Pike mounted his horse half an hour later, he said, "If you can stay awake, find a good position near the entrance to the canyon. It's not that big, and if what Charlie told me about where this place was is true, it's the only place they could really come at you."

"Yes, sir," both young men said.

"And I'll talk to Charlie to see if we can get you some relief out here."

"That'd be welcome," Blake said.

"Can't promise you nothin'." Pike mounted his sorrel. "And don't be derelict about your duties again, boys. I just might come back and check on you of a night. I find you've been neglectful. I won't be so forgivin' as I was tonight." With that, he rode off.

Pike headed back to the McAllister place, went into the barn, tended his horse, and stretched out on a bed of new hay. Though he was glad Marcy was not about to interrupt him since it was so late, he found he did miss her — and the pie.

The young woman was not happy with him at breakfast the next morning, but there was nothing he could — or would — do about it.

"You got a couple boys could relieve Vin and Arch, Charlie?"

"A problem?" McAllister looked a little worried. He also looked tired, Pike thought.

Pike shook his head. "Nah. I just figure that if it's only the two of 'em out there, they might get a little lax. Rotate the teams out there every few days if you can."

"I'll see what I can arrange. Won't be easy, though."

"Nothin' is easy these days, Charlie. Nothin' is."

McAllister nodded sadly.

"How're things comin' along here?"

"Good as can be, I reckon. We got the stream, so water's no concern, but we'll need to make another run into town tomorrow, I reckon. Need supplies, and arms and ammunition like you suggested."

"I'll ride along like last time, though I doubt we'll have any trouble. I'm pretty certain Hungerford's heard about his men by now and has sent for more and is waitin' on 'em. 'Course, if he's done that, they may be here tomorrow, but I'd like to think not."

"We'll be leavin' early."

"I wouldn't expect otherwise. I'll be ready."

"Oh, and Brodie, you'll be havin' some company in the barn soon. Several of the other men'll have to bunk in there with you."

Out of the corner of his eye, Pike saw that Marcy almost dropped a large coffeepot when she heard that. "Just tell 'em to leave their boots on so their foot stink doesn't keep me awake." Everyone laughed — except Marcy.

Pike made his usual circuit around the area and saw nothing to indicate that Hungerford and the cattlemen's association were planning anything imminently. He decided not to check on Vin and Arch, figuring they'd still be all right.

Finally, he headed for the McAllister place, tended his horse, and went to supper at the house. He tried to avoid Marcy's gaze but was only partly successful since he could feel her eyes on him throughout the meal, which did little to improve his appetite.

He wasn't surprised when she showed up at the barn that evening. She didn't bother to knock, and she was obviously unhappy, but she had brought some cobbler. Pike figured it was so in case someone questioned why she was outside, she would have an excuse. "Hope you like it," she said in a tone that was somewhat less than friendly.

"Might. If I had some sociable company."

"Harrumph." But Marcy sat on a crate. "Where were you the last few nights?"

"None of your concern, miss. I had men's business to take care of."

Marcy pouted. "But I missed seein' you."

Pike was tired of this. The stress of the past few weeks and the worry about the next few were wearing on him. He had flirted with the girl for a short spell, but he now regretted it. It had meant far more to her than to him, and it had led her to believe he had as much feeling for her as she apparently had for him. "I've missed sittin' with you, too, Marcy, but you've read too much into these few evenings."

"But . . ."

She stopped when he waved her into silence. He rose and headed quietly to the door. Cracking it open a couple of inches, he peered out for some moments. Shaking his head, he went back to where Marcy still sat.

"You best get back to the house, Marcy."

"But why?"

"I think I heard someone outside. I'm not sure, but I saw a shadow like someone movin' quickly toward the house."

"You're just sayin' that so I'll leave," she whined.

"No, I'm not. If there was someone out there, it might not go well for you if you get back to the house too much later. The cobbler was a good reason to be out, but it's not such a good reason to be out so long. Now, go on. We'll talk again another time."

CHAPTER 15

It was barely daylight when they pulled out: Charlie McAllister, his son Matt, and Len Blake, one of the other small ranchers in the area. Pike left before the others, heading down the road to Graystone. Half a mile later, he headed off the trail, riding slowly parallel to the road toward Hungerford's ranch. The spread was quiet, and what few gunmen were around were just waking up and sitting outside the bunkhouse drinking coffee and puffing on cigarettes. He wished he had spent a bit more time at breakfast. Some more coffee and another biscuit or two would've been nice.

With a sigh, he moseyed on, searching for anything that would suggest danger to him or the others. It was a boring day, with no sign of trouble.

As he had the last time, Pike waited among the trees on the hillside beyond the stream. He breathed a sigh of relief when

McAllister pulled out with the wagon loaded with all manner of supplies.

Pike remained where he was for an hour after McAllister left, wanting to make sure the wagon wasn't followed. He was glad he did. Just as he was preparing to leave, he spotted Marshal Uriah Haney heading in the same direction as McAllister. Pike rode up the hill and across the crest, kept to the trees for a couple of miles, then stopped and waited.

Before long, Haney hove into sight. Pike fired a shot inches in front of the marshal's horse. Haney stopped abruptly as the horse snorted and stutter-stepped a little.

"That's as far as you go, Haney. Turn back."

"If I don't, are you gonna shoot me?" the marshal said with a distinct sneer in his voice.

"I'd rather not." He left the rest of the threat unsaid but obvious.

"You'd never get away with it."

"Sure I would. Nobody knows you're here, and nobody'll know who did it. Your carcass'll lay there 'til some poor spirit stumbles over it."

"I told my deputy where I was going." Haney did not sound as certain anymore.

"You don't have a deputy, and even if you

did, he'd more than likely not give a hoot or holler about you. He'd just have his eye on your job."

"Other folks know I was goin' to see Charlie McAllister."

"Your pile of horse manure is growin' bigger by the second. You were goin' to Hungerford's place to tell him that McAllister bought some guns and ammo to protect themselves."

"No, I wasn't. I . . ."

"Go on back to town, Marshal. Keep your mouth shut, and you might come out of this whole affair still breathin'."

"What affair?"

"Foolish question, Haney. There's a war comin', and it will be hard and bloody. A yellow-belly like you won't stand a chance."

"I'll be fine when I join the Cattlemen's Association as one of their range detectives."

Pike laughed. "You'll die before you even clear leather the first time you face a real shootist." He grew serious again. "Go back to town, Marshal. Now! Or you'll never see the sunset."

Haney sat there for a few moments, trying to act brave, then turned his horse. "You'll pay for this, whoever you are." He thought he knew, and it did not make him the least bit comfortable.

Pike watched as Haney rode slowly down the road, but he did not move for another half-hour, wanting to be sure the marshal was not coming back this way. Then he headed toward the Hungerford ranch in case Haney had followed some other trail up over the mountain to it, but there was no sign the marshal had gone another way, so Pike finally headed to what had become his home.

As he rode up to the house, he noticed several rifles protruding from windows. He smiled, pleased to see the people taking precautions.

"About time you showed up," McAllister said with a shaky grin. "Viv said she wouldn't hold supper for you more than a few minutes."

"I'm obliged. Let me tend my horse, and I'll be in directly."

"Abe'll take care of it. Come on in and set at the table. Abe, come on out and tend Mr. Pike's horse."

"I heard ya, Pa," the youth grumbled good-naturedly.

Pike sat down to a heaping bowl of beef stew with biscuits, fresh-churned butter, and hot coffee. "A fine, fine meal, ma'am," he said as he sat back, sated, with another cup of coffee. The women adjourned to another room, and the men gathered around the table. As usual, McAllister sat across from Pike. He looked sad and angry.

"Something stuck in your craw, Charlie?"

"As Chuck and Willard Mathews were headin' here, someone took some shots at 'em. Didn't hit 'em but killed one of the mules pulling the wagon. Willard had to walk to Axel Morgan's place to get help, and he was scared down to his boots on the trip, figurin' he could be gunned down any second."

"A reasonable thought. Since they didn't kill any of the men, it was just another way to put the fear of God — well, the fear of Hungerford, who I expect thinks of himself as God — into you. Keep you on edge."

"It's workin'," Felder said.

Pike nodded sadly.

"What about you, Brodie? Any trouble on the way?" McAllister asked.

"Nothin' to speak of. Marshal Haney started followin' you down the road, but I think he was headin' to Hungerford's. I discouraged him from doing so."

"You didn't kill him, did you?" McAllister asked, suddenly worried.

"Nope. Just warned him off."

"Think he'll heed the warnin'?"

Pike shrugged. "Can't say. I think so, but

he's such a horse's ass that I can't tell."

"Do you consider him a threat?"

"No. Even if he was to join up with Hungerford — and it's mighty doubtful Hungerford would take him on — he'd not be of much consequence."

"Good. Now what?"

"Keep on getting' ready. It's been a few days, and if Hungerford is waitin' on new recruits, I figure they'll be gettin' here soon. We best be ready."

"We will be," McAllister said firmly. "What'll you be doin'?"

"Keepin' an eye out for when the gunmen do show up."

"Wouldn't just killin' Hungerford end our troubles?" Matt McAllister asked. "His gunmen wouldn't come against us if he's not around to pay them, I would reckon."

"True, but there's nothin' to stop the others in the association from payin' 'em. And if they know I — we — killed Hungerford, they might not show any restraint and take their chances with the law, even federal law, by attackin' here straight on."

"Hadn't thought about that."

"Wouldn't expect you to." Pike pushed himself up. "Well, I suppose I best be getting' some shuteye. Night, folks."

"Night. Oh, and your company in the

barn has arrived."

Pike grimaced, then shrugged and left. The others, though, seemed wary of him. They were friends of McAllister, so mostly small ranchers and not used to a man who lived by the gun. They kept their distance, which suited Pike just fine.

Breakfast was a rather chaotic affair, with all the new faces crowding into the dining area. Pike took one look at the madness and went back outside. Waiting a bit seemed like a good idea, though that might mean the food would be gone when he went back inside, he thought.

He remained outside, sitting on a bench just outside the door, enjoying the day. It was something he had not done in a while. It was going to be a warm day, but he could sense that autumn was not far off. He looked forward to that, but not to the winter that would follow.

Marcy sidled up beside him, plate in one hand, cup in the other. "It's busy inside, so I thought you'd like to eat out here." She smiled brightly.

"Obliged," he said as he took the plate of biscuits and gravy with bacon on the side. He rested the plate on his knees and ate hungrily as Marcy placed the coffee next to him.

"Won't you be missed inside?" he asked between bites.

"There's plenty of women in there to handle what's needed. I don't think they'll even know I'm not there." She plunked down beside him.

Pike was well aware that Marcy was inching closer to him, and he smiled to himself. She apparently thought she was doing so surreptitiously. Finally, she was just about brushing his side.

"That was good," he said, finishing the food. He sipped the coffee.

"You want more?"

"There enough for everyone?"

"Yep." She hopped up, grabbed his plate and cup, and hurried back inside.

Pike watched her. She was, he thought, quite a lovely, shapely woman. His mind drifted to the possibilities, but he shook his head to clear those musings. It would not work, he told himself firmly. He could not give her what she wanted — or what she thought she wanted, at least not in the way she saw it. He expected she wanted him to take her away from the drab life of living on a small ranch, never quite rich enough to afford fine things, facing the thought of marrying someone who was from the same sort of family as hers. She would want him to take her away from the terror and torture that she and all the others were going through. She did not realize she would be jumping into an even harsher life with him.

Marcy was back in a few minutes and was a little more obvious in perching next to him.

Despite his misgivings, he did not say anything, just tried to tell himself that it meant nothing to him. To his annoyance, he found the closeness pleasing.

Pike finished the food before long and drained the last of the coffee, then handed the plate and cup to Marcy. "That was a right fine meal, Marcy."

"Thank you," she responded with a blush. She didn't want to spoil the moment by telling him she had not made it.

"Well," he said, rising, "I'd best be on my way."

"You'll be back tonight?" she asked anxiously.

"Yep. Unless something happens. Now, go on inside and help the other women clean up. Don't want your ma givin' you trouble for wastin' your time servin' some saddle tramp."

Marcy giggled. She looked for a moment as if she wanted to kiss him, but she turned and ran inside.

Pike again watched for a moment, then headed for the barn. "Just keep those thoughts out of your mind, boy," he muttered to himself.

He saddled his horse and rode out toward Hungerford's ranch. Seeing nothing out of the ordinary, he turned toward the canyon where the herd was being kept.

As he rode cautiously into the canyon, he spotted Arch Blake peering out from behind a boulder high on the cliff. He smiled when Blake called, "Identify yourself!"

Pike took off his hat. It's me, Arch. Brodie Pike."

"Howdy, Mr. Pike. Vin is over where you first found us. Likely asleep after he had the earlier watch."

But he wasn't. He was waiting for Pike, and the latter figured he had heard Blake.

"Things all right?" Pike asked as he dismounted.

"Boring, mostly."

"That's a good thing, considerin'. You haven't been relieved yet by others, I reckon?"

"Nope."

"Charlie says he'll get some others out here soon as he can."

"Hope it's soon," Mathews said, then blanched a little. "Sorry, Mr. Pike. I didn't mean . . ."

"I know what you meant, and I'd feel the same were I you. This isn't great duty."

Mathews nodded, relieved. "I was just about to have a bite before takin' my rest. Care to join me?"

"Long as it won't put you out none or leave you short."

"Got plenty. Be glad to have some different company from Arch," he said with a laugh.

CHAPTER 16

Pike stood on the hill overlooking the town of Graystone. He had been here for a while but remained patient. The stage was due any minute now, and Pike wanted to see who the new arrivals were if any. This was his third day of doing so, but so far, no one suspicious had arrived. That did not change on this day.

He waited until all the passengers had left the coach, then he turned his horse and rode up over the mountain through the heavy stand of pines and aspens. He soon rode down onto the road, where he could make better time.

Before long, he sensed there was someone coming toward him. He swiftly pulled off into the trees and partway up the heavily treed slope, pulled to a stop well behind cover, and waited.

Within minutes, Ulysses Hungerford rode into view, surrounded by five watchful gunmen. "I'll be damned," Pike muttered. He rode back the way he had come, toward Graystone and took his position again overlooking the town.

He did not have to wait long before Hungerford and his men entered the town and stopped in front of the Mountain Air hotel. After he dismounted he entered the building. One of his men took the reins of the cattleman's horse, and all five of them rode down to the stables.

Pike remained there for a little while, but he soon decided that nothing was going to happen today and headed for the McAllister place again. Before he got there, though, he cut across the ranch land to the northwest, wanting to take a look at the house that had been shared by the Blake and Mathews families. It was the farthest one from the McAllister place and the most likely to be susceptible to burning.

The house was still intact, though it was full of bullet holes, all the windows were broken, and a dozen chickens lay around the place, all shot dead. "Dammit," Pike muttered.

By the time he arrived back at the McAllister place, it was dark, and he sat down to a late supper by himself, being waited on diligently by Marcy McAllister. He told the men what he and found at the Blake/ Mathews place, which angered them all.

"This has got to end soon, Brodie," McAllister said in a voice tight with anger and worry.

"I know, Charlie."

Pike headed to the barn and laid down on his bedroll. Marcy had enough sense not to visit him, for which he was grateful.

After a hearty breakfast, he headed east instead of toward Graystone or Hungerford's ranch. The stage would not arrive in the town until later in the afternoon, and he doubted anything would be going on at the latter unless Hungerford had decided to ride back to his ranch at night, which Pike thought would have been foolish. That meant there were likely only a couple of his hired guns left at the ranch. They would be there to keep watch on the property, Pike figured. He was wrong.

As he neared the Blake/Mathews place, he could see smoke in the distance. He kicked the horse into a gallop, and within minutes, he was close enough to the house to see two men on horseback watching the flames. He thought they were laughing. He urged a bit more speed out of the horse and pulled his Winchester from the saddle scabbard. He wished he had his sniper rifle, the .52-caliber

Sharps with the full copper scope that he had used in the Civil War, but he had stored it in the barn, unknown to anyone but him.

The two men became aware of him and raced east toward the mountain. Pike pulled his horse up sharply and jumped out of the saddle. Kneeling, he aimed and fired the rifle. He thought he saw one man flinch and figured he'd hit him, but if he had, it was not fatally.

"Damn," he snapped. He put the Winchester away and rode a little closer to the house. The place was engulfed. There would be no saving it even if there were several men and plenty of water available. With a sad shake of his head, he went back to the road leading to Graystone, riding cautiously. He was fairly sure why Hungerford had ridden into town the day before, but he could be wrong, and he didn't want to run into him or his men on the road. He supposed that if such an encounter were to take place, he could try to kill Hungerford and however many of his men. Even if he was gunned down in return, it might solve the problem for the McAllisters, but he doubted it. The Cattlemen's Association would likely retaliate, as he had warned Felder.

He pulled up in the trees on the far side of the hill and loosened the horse's cinch, then let it free to graze. Pike sat and ate some biscuits and a slice of cold ham from breakfast. A couple of hours later, he tightened the cinch and rode over the crest of the hill through the pines and took up his usual spot looking out over Graystone. Minutes later it started to rain, though not very heavily. He pulled on his slicker.

The stage was a little late today, arriving more than half an hour after its scheduled time. When it stopped, Hungerford and his men were waiting under the portico of the hotel. Six hard-looking, well-heeled men disembarked from the stage and were greeted by Hungerford.

Pike thought one looked familiar, so he pulled out his collapsible telescope and surveyed the newcomers. As he had thought, he recognized one of the men, a bounty hunter and sometime ally named Abel Farnum. That perplexed him a bit. He hated to see an acquaintance throw in with Hungerford, but at the same time, it might give Pike a chance to get some inside information about Hungerford's plans by playing on that friendship.

He waited a little longer, but they had all gone into the hotel, and Pike figured they were in town for the night. He mounted up and rode out.

He had a rough night, worrying some about approaching Farnum. While they knew each other, Farnum was working for Hungerford, and it might be difficult to get close enough to him to pump him for information. Farnum might also be unwilling to talk against his new boss. He was tired and grumpy at breakfast, speaking little. He finished quickly, wrapped some biscuits and ham in a piece of cloth, and stuffed the parcel into a saddlebag when he got to the barn. He saddled the animal and rode out.

He headed toward Hungerford's ranch, but to the southeast side instead of his usual spot on the southwest. That would give him a better look at the road leading to the ranch. He tied the horse to a hackberry bush, sat with his back resting against a tree, and waited. The rain of yesterday had stopped, but it was still overcast and humid. It made him sleepy, and he soon dozed off.

He awoke with a start when he heard people coming down the road leading to the ranch. He rose, pulled out his spyglass, and spotted a new man riding alongside Hungerford. He was obviously not a gunman, so Pike figured he was one of the other cattlemen.

Three men who had been loitering in

front of the house, one of them wearing a sling, moved out to meet the newcomers. Two of them took the horses from Hungerford and his crony. Hungerford spoke to the man wearing the sling, and he did not seem pleased with the response. Pike figured it was the man he had shot at the Mathews place. The bodyguards dismounted and led their own horses to the barn while the two bosses entered the house.

This did not look good to Pike. A meeting between Hungerford and one of his associates indicated a planning session and the fact that he counted thirteen gunmen meant trouble. He waited a while longer, but it did not seem as if anything would happen today, so he swung into the saddle and rode off quickly. Late that day, he arrived at the canyon where the young men — Vin Mathews and Arch Blake having been replaced by Willard Mathews, Vin's brother, and Claude Dickson — were watching the cattle to check on them. Everything seemed to be all right.

"Make sure you boys stay on the alert," Pike said as he remounted after talking to the youths for a bit.

"You expectin' trouble?" Dickson asked, a little nervous.

"Always do. But I don't think anything is

looming. You just need to keep a close eye out."

Both young men nodded.

It was dark by the time Pike made it back to the McAllister place. He went straight to the barn to tend to his horse, then headed to the house. Charlie McAllister was waiting for him on the porch. "You look tired, Brodie," he said.

"Reckon I am."

"Come on in. Food'll help you."

Pike nodded and followed McAllister into the house. Marcy and her mother were already setting plates and a mug of coffee on the table. "Obliged, ladies," Pike said as he sat and started shoveling food in.

McAllister gave him some time to eat, then said, "It seems like you've got information."

"Yep. And it ain't good." He took another bite of beefsteak and swallowed, then said, "The new gunmen have arrived. With the men already there, I counted thirteen."

"That sure don't sound good."

"It ain't," Pike said flatly. "And makin' it worse, one of Hungerford's cronies — at least, I think it was one of the other cattlemen — rode in with Hungerford. I figure they're plannin' what to do."

McAllister took a while before asking,

"Did you get a look at him?" When Pike nodded, McAllister went on, "What'd this fellow look like?"

"A little taller and heftier than Hungerford, at least on horseback. Well-dressed in a fancy checked suit. Derby. Long set of whiskers."

"He's one of Hungerford's pals, all right. Miles Appleyard. Mostly stays to himself far as I know. Leaves things to Hungerford."

"Know anything about him or the other cattlemen?" Pike finished his coffee, and Marcy immediately refilled his mug. He nodded thanks but did not see her beam in pride.

"Not much. Barrington lives in the southeast corner of Buckskin County. He's about the farthest from Graystone and Hungerford. Appleyard and Forsythe have ranches on the other side of Graystone. I think Barrington's more of a money man than a rancher."

Pike nodded absent-mindedly.

"What should we do now?"

"It'd be a good time to post sentries like we talked about. I'm hoping we still have some time before anything happens, but if we do, it won't be much."

"But with the new gunmen here and Hungerford meeting with Appleyard, won't they be comin' here soon?" Connor Felder asked.

"Could be, but I figure that Hungerford will want to meet with the others before he does anything. I could be wrong."

"And if you are?" Felder asked.

"Then we're all in a deep pile of . . . manure."

"Time's runnin' out," McAllister mused more than said.

"It is," Pike acknowledged. "You folks still have time to pull up stakes and move on."

"That what you're suggestin' now?" Clay Dunn snapped.

"Ain't suggestin' anything. Just sayin' that if you decide that's what's best, now'd be time to kick up the dust."

"No," McAllister said firmly. "We'll make a stand here. That right, Viv?" He looked at his wife.

"It is." There was a slight tremor in her voice, but determination, too.

Pike grinned tightly. "Figured you'd say something like that, Charlie." He paused. "I know one of the gun hands who arrived yesterday. If I can contact him, maybe I can learn something of their plans."

"Think that's likely?"

"Don't know. I don't know if I can get close enough to him by himself to talk to him. And if I do, there's no guarantee he'll want to cross his boss."

"That would be real trouble," Felder said.

"It would, but I reckon not much more than we're already in."

After breakfast the next morning, Viv McAllister handed Pike a small sack with some hard-cooked eggs, cold roast beef, and cornbread.

"Thank you, ma'am," Pike said before heading to the barn, saddling his horse and riding out. He pushed hard, taking a road around Graystone until he came to a ranch that he assumed belonged to either Appleyard or Forsythe, based on the site and relative splendor of the abode. It was in a large valley, so there was no place for Pike to hide and keep an eye on the place. He gave the ranch house a wide berth and moved on until he found the ranch that belonged to the other cattlemen's association member. This was even tougher to watch since it sat on a small hump of land and commanded a good view around it.

Using his telescope, he determined that there were no more than one or two gunmen at the location and everything seemed calm. He rode back to the other baronial manse and checked that as best he could with his telescope. That, too, seemed to be inactive for the most part.

He headed home.

CHAPTER 17

McAllister and the others were a little more agitated than usual when Pike got back in the afternoon. He asked about it when he stopped near the men in the yard a little in front of the house.

"Couple of fellas stopped by saying they were lookin' to buy some cattle. Didn't believe 'em for a minute."

"Why?"

" 'Cause they looked like you, dammit," Clay Dunn said.

"What's that mean?" Pike asked, looking askance at Dunn.

"They were heeled, and they didn't look like no ranchers or even cattle brokers."

Pike looked at McAllister, who nodded. "They were packin' guns and looked like they knew how to use 'em. Weren't the friendliest-lookin' fellas either. One of 'em looked like he'd been in a few too many fistfights and lost many of 'em."

"Reckon they were hopin' you'd tell 'em where you're hidin' the cattle, or at least have you head there to get 'em, convinced you could sell 'em. Those scum would follow."

"My thinkin' too," McAllister said. "I kindly told 'em we had no cattle, and they should try Hungerford's place." He looked nervous but pleased with himself.

"You did well, Charlie, but I don't think them comin' here bodes well." Pike stood still, thinking.

"What should we do, Brodie?"

"You folks? Nothing."

"Nothing?" McAllister asked as he, Dunn, and even Connor Felder looked at him in question.

Pike said, "This is my business, and I'll see to it." His voice had taken on a hard edge.

"I'm goin' with you," Dunn said.

"Like hell you are," Pike spat.

"Afraid I'll find out you're really in cahoots with those men?"

"Nope. I'm worried you'll get both of us killed because you're such an ass."

"Shut up, Clay," McAllister ordered before the young man could say anything more.

"Mind if I come along, Mr. Pike?" Felder asked.

"Got a death wish?"

"Nope. Nor do I think you're in cahoots with those boys and I need to keep an eye on you. I just think it's time I did something to actually help."

"You're plenty of help here, Con," McAllister said.

"Maybe, but it doesn't seem that way. Besides, Mr. Pike saved our bacon over to Graystone not so long ago. Least I can do is try to back him up when he confronts those two."

"Might be dangerous," Pike said.

"I know that."

"You know how to use a six-shooter?"

"Some. Not as good as you or those boys, of course, but I might be of some help."

Pike almost grinned but didn't. "You think you can kill a man?"

Felder shrugged. "Don't know, but that might be expected of all of us should the cattlemen send their forces against us."

"Saddle up, then. We'll leave as soon as you're ready." He wasn't sure he wouldn't regret this, but he understood Felder's desire to prove himself.

"Yes, sir." Felder hurried off.

"How long ago did they leave, Charlie?"

"An hour or so, maybe. Left heading southwest toward the hill yonder."

"Road on the other side leads toward the area south of Graystone, doesn't it?"

"Reckon so. Doesn't matter, does it?"

"Only if they're heading to the ranch of one of Hungerford's partners."

"Damn."

"Might not matter. If they haven't been gone long, we should be able to catch up to 'em before they get anywhere near one of those ranches unless they're ridin' like hell."

"They weren't when they left here. Don't mean they didn't start as soon as they got out of sight."

"Could be, but I doubt it. I reckon they're gonna stay in the vicinity, hopin' you might send someone to warn whoever's watchin' the cattle."

"Then you better get a move on," McAllister said with a grim smile.

"Soon as Connor's ready."

"Good." McAllister paused. "No, wait. You need something to eat. I reckon you haven't had much other than that small sack of things Viv gave you this mornin'."

"Don't have time, but if she's got something ready that we can take with us, that'd be good."

"Done. Clay, go tell Viv to make up a satchel of vittles for Brodie and Connor."

Dunn looked like he was about to argue,

but he thought better of it and hurried into the house.

Minutes later, Marcy McAllister handed Pike a burlap sack. "Some sausages and a few baked taters, but no butter," she said apologetically.

"This'll be fine. Tell your ma I said thanks." He climbed on his horse as Felder arrived. "Let's ride," Pike said.

A few minutes later, Felder asked, "Why're we takin' the road to Graystone? They were headed up over the hill."

"And they might be sittin' just on the other side of the hill keepin' watch."

"Oh."

"Don't think bad of yourself. You've not done anything like this before. We'll go down the road a little way and see if they did eventually come this way. If we figure they haven't, we'll turn up the hill. If they're there, we might come up behind 'em and get the drop on 'em." He smiled a little and opened the food sack. "Here, have something to eat."

"Must be a hard life, doin' what you do," Felder said as he munched on a sausage.

"Can be, I reckon. Doesn't seem so most times. I've been doin' this a long time, and I don't hardly think about it much anymore. 'Cept when things go bad."

"Like bein' shot?"

Pike smiled crookedly. "That does put things in a different light."

"You were hurt bad that time before you came back here, weren't you?"

If he was a less-hardened man, Pike might have shivered at the remembrance. As it was, he shook his head at the thought of having been taken down. "It was bad, for certain. Worst I ever had done to me."

"You were shot more than that one time?"

Pike offered him a rueful smile. "Couple times. None nearly as bad as that time, though."

"Must hurt like hell."

"Yep, though sometimes it takes a little while. The shock of bein' hit kind of numbs you to the pain for a time. But when it hits, it's bad."

After finishing their meal, they sped up and rode at a good clip for perhaps half an hour. Then Pike took them off the road onto the tree-covered slope. They moved slowly then, snaking through the pines. Felder started to ask something, but Pike shushed him with a wave of the hand.

The bounty hunter stopped them every few minutes and sat there listening. Hearing nothing but the creak of leather, the tinkling of bridles and bits, and the breeze soughing through the trees, he would move on. Finally, though, Pike picked up the sounds of men talking. They were still a little way off, but it was audible. He dismounted, indicating Felder should do the same. The two tied their horses loosely to branches.

As they moved cautiously forward on foot, Pike did not see a need to warn Felder to be quiet, even though the man was not used to such activity. Pike was surprised when his companion picked his way through the forest even more noiselessly than he did.

Suddenly a man, six-gun in hand, loomed up before them. "Lookin' for something, folks?" he asked.

"We're huntin'," Pike said hastily. "Thought we saw a deer up this way."

"Hard to hunt deer with two holstered revolvers."

"Makes it a challenge," Felder said nervously.

The gunman turned his eyes toward Felder, almost amused. It was enough for Pike to yank out a six-gun and put a bullet through the gunman's head.

"Stay here," Pike snapped at Felder, who ducked behind a chokecherry bush. Pike moved swiftly and smoothly to his left as he heard men coming through the trees. He stopped behind a thick spruce and waited.

Two men came running from a small glade, pistols in hand, calling, "Lou! Lou!"

"He's dead," Pike said from behind cover.

Both men whirled. They were good, un-afraid, and seemed to know where the voice had come from. Both fired, their bullets thudding into the spruce, keeping Pike from returning fire.

From his hiding place behind the bush, Connor Felder drew his pistol and shakily let go a shot in the general direction of the two men.

"What the hell?" one of them said, spin-ning toward where the shot had come from.

The other looked that way for a moment, then looked back at the tree where Pike had been hiding — and took two bullets in the chest for his effort.

Pike fired at the man who had been searching for whoever had shot at him and his partner. The bullet caught the man in the back, knocking him down. He dropped his pistol as he fell.

"Stay there, Connor," Pike said as he came out from behind the tree. He checked the man he had shot first here and made sure he was dead. He started reloading his revolver as he walked to the other man, who lay groaning, alive but in serious pain and likely not to live much longer. Using his boot, Pike rolled the man over on his back. "Who're you workin' for?" he asked, voice harsh.

"Go to hell," the man gasped.

"Likely will one day, but you'll be there long before I arrive. Now, who're you workin' for?"

"Ain't gonna say." He tried to smile but could only manage a grimace. "What're you gonna do, kill me?"

"I could do that and put you out of your misery. Or I could just let you lay there and bleed to death."

The man gasped for breath, then asked, "You'll kill me quick?"

"Yep."

"We were hired by a fella named Appleyard. Said he was a member of the Buckskin County Cattlemen's Association."

"What for?"

"Wanted us to find out where the rustlers were keepin' their stolen cattle."

"You ever think that the cattle might not've been rustled?"

"Didn't matter. Appleyard said they were rustled, and we were to find 'em."

"Didn't work out well for you, did it?"

But the man had died.

"Connor, go get these men's horses and

bring 'em here."

"What're you gonna do?" Felder asked when he had brought the three saddled horses up.

"Send 'em home, in a manner of speaking."

Felder decided not to ask more questions for the time being.

Pike and Felder tossed the dead men over their saddles and tied them down. While Pike finished, Felder got his and Pike's horses. They mounted, and with the corpse-laden horses in tow, headed southeast. They stopped at the rim of trees along the meadow in which Miles Appleyard's big ranch house sat.

Pike untied the three horses from each other, then sent them on their way with a short, sharp smack on the rump of each one. The animals bolted across the grassy sward.

"Time to go home," Pike said.

CHAPTER 18

It was well after dark when Pike and Felder arrived back at the McAllister place, but most everyone was still up. As Felder dismounted, his wife, Becca, rushed to him and fiercely wrapped her arms around him. In return, he enfolded her in his arms and stroked her hair.

"You had me scared half to death, Connor Felder," Becca said, her voice holding a mix of fear and anger. "Don't you ever go and do something like that again."

"This ain't the time or place, Becca," Felder said in embarrassment.

"Like the devil, it isn't." But she gave him one more hug, then took his hand and led him toward the house. "Dinner's cold, but I'll reheat it for you."

Watching the others' smiles of fondness and amusement at the couple, Pike felt a strong surge of sadness, even emptiness. Only once had he had such a relationship with a woman, one in which she loved him so much she was willing to let him do what he thought was necessary despite her being filled with fear for him. It ended poorly.

"Abe, take care of Connor's and Mr. Pike's horses. Come on inside, Brodie. Viv'll be happy to heat up some supper for you too."

"I'll do it," Marcy exclaimed and hurried into the house.

McAllister seemed a bit surprised by Marcy's eagerness and glanced at Pike to see his reaction. The bounty hunter had a small, sad smile on his face, making McAllister wonder all the more.

Pike dismounted and handed the reins of his sorrel to Abe, McAllister's youngest son, and followed the clan's leader into the house. Marcy was not alone in hurrying to provide a meal for the two new arrivals, but she made sure she served Pike. She smiled in relief and hopefulness as she placed a plate of beefsteak and potatoes in front of him.

"Thanks, Marcy," Pike said as he dug in. As he ate and drank, he began to wonder about the young woman. Could she provide the kind of relationship Becca had with Connor and Viv had with Charlie? he wondered. He sighed inwardly. It would never come to be, he figured. Considering his profession, there was no way he could provide a proper life for her. The thought of giving up his wandering, violence-filled life never really entered his mind. He was what he was, and he could not see another way for him.

"So, what happened?" McAllister asked as he took a seat across the table from Pike and Felder. Clay Dunn, Matt McAllister, Claude Morgan, Chuck Mathews, and Len Blake, all neighbors with small ranches nearby, gathered around, interested.

"Not much to tell," Pike said around mouthfuls of food, his voice flat. "We found 'em. They won't bother us again."

"It was that easy?" Matt McAllister asked, surprised.

Pike shrugged and took a sip of coffee.

"No, it wasn't," Felder said. "There was another man we didn't know about. Pike shot him before he could fire at us. Then the other two came runnin' up and started blazin' away. Brodie took care of 'em while I hid behind a bush." He blushed in embarrassment.

"That right?" Charlie McAllister asked.

"Not quite," Pike said a little sourly. "It wasn't for Connor, we might both be pushin' up daisies."

"I didn't do nothin'," Felder said, surprised, and his wife looked on in horror.

"You hadn't distracted them boys at the right time, I might not've been able to take care of things. I was a damn fool for not considerin' there might be more than the two we knew about."

"But . . ." Felder started.

"Thanks for the meal, ladies," Pike growled as he shoved the plate away, stood, and stomped out, angry at himself.

In doing so, he did not hear Clay Dunn say, "I always knew he was a danger to us all."

Nor did he see Felder rise and punch Dunn in the jaw hard enough to drop the man unconscious.

Marcy ignored as best she could the stares of surprise and wonder of the men staying in the barn when she entered with a coffeepot in one hand, a mug dangling from a finger and a plate with a healthy helping of apple cobbler in the other. She went straight to where Pike was sitting on a hay bale.

He was ready to say something, but she ordered, "Don't say a word, Brodie, unless it's thanks."

"Thanks, ma'am," he muttered.

"That's better," Marcy said as she handed

him the plate of cobbler.

"Don't we get some too, delivered by a fine gal like you?" one of the men called, getting chuckles from the others.

"You just watch your words, Axel Morgan," Marcy said. "It wasn't you who went out there to confront those bad men."

"Yes'm." He and the other men went back to playing cards.

"You didn't have to do this, Marcy," Pike said.

"Just hush like I told you and eat your cobbler." She placed the mug on the bale and filled it with coffee, then set the coffeepot on the floor and sat on the bale, the steaming mug between the two.

"You didn't have to . . ."

"Eat!"

"You sure are a bossy woman."

"Yes, I am." She flushed.

Pike was disconcerted by Marcy's closeness. Not that he hadn't been physically close to women before, but there was an emotional context here that was unusual for him, and he wasn't sure what, if anything, he should do about it. So, he did nothing but eat. When he finished, he placed the plate alongside the cup. "Thank you, Marcy. That was some good."

"I'm glad."

Before either of them could say anything else, Charlie McAllister appeared in the barn doorway. "There you are, Marcy," he said, though not too harshly. "Your ma's lookin' for you. She's worried."

"Sorry, Papa. I just brought Mr. Pike some cobbler. He left the house so quickly he didn't get any."

"Is he done?" His tone had sharpened a little.

"I am," Pike snapped. "She's done nothin' wrong. Neither of us has."

"I didn't say that."

"You implied as much. She was bein' kind and thoughtful."

"That's not the way some see it."

"Like who?"

"It's not your concern. Marcy, get back to the house."

As Marcy began gathering the coffeepot and the rest, Pike rose and walked to the stall where his horse was. He tossed a saddle blanket on the sorrel's back, then grabbed the saddle from where it sat on the wood partition between the stalls and set that on the animal, too.

"What're you doin'?" McAllister asked, surprised.

"Leavin'. There's no call for me to stand between family members. If I'm makin' things uncomfortable for you and Viv because Marcy brought me a sweet and some coffee, then it's time for me to move on."

"Papa, you can't let him leave," Marcy said with a quaver in her voice.

"Go on back to the house, Marcy," McAllister ordered, though he sounded somewhat contrite.

Marcy hurried out, casting a nervous glance behind her.

"Rest of you boys need to go take a stroll and catch some evenin' air."

The other men headed out, curious about what was going to happen in the barn but not wanting to annoy McAllister more than he was.

"Stop what you're doin', Brodie. Please." He strode toward the stall where Pike was. "As a father, I got to care for my little girl."

Pike simply nodded.

"Her ma's worried about her, too."

Pike nodded again.

"You're a hard man, footloose, a wanderer. You don't have any roots. You hunt men for a livin', usin' your gun. I expect when we get through these doin's here, you'll be movin' on."

"If I ain't dead," Pike said with a grim smile.

"There is that. All the rest of us might be

dead, too, but if we ain't, you'll be movin' on, I figure."

"Likely."

"Knowin' that, I don't want you plantin' ideas in Marcy's head about stayin' on here with her and settlin' down. As a father, I can't let that happen."

"Like any good father," Pike said. "But I ain't leadin' her to think such. I think she might be infatuated with me, though I can't figure out why."

"You're not an ordinary fella. You're not one of the boys around here, small ranchers without much wanderlust about 'em. She sees a world of adventure, places she'll never have a chance to see anyway else. Maybe a little danger along the way. She can't see the loneliness, the real danger of you gettin' gunned down, leavin' her adrift in a world she ain't prepared for."

"You're right."

"Marcy ain't like Viv and Becca and the others. They're down to earth, always have been."

"You sure of that?" Pike asked with a small grin.

McAllister thought that over for a bit, then nodded. "I believe so. At least, they seem happy with their lot, tough as it can be sometimes. But Marcy's always been a mite flighty, dreamin' of things she can't ever have."

"She's kind of like a spirited horse. You don't want to be mean and break it, but you do need to gentle it."

"That sounds about right. Viv and I don't want to break her spirit, but she's got to get these wild ideas out of her head."

"Bein' hard on her might not be the right way to go about it. But I ain't no expert on women, and maybe that's the way to go. I don't think you should be too hard on her."

"We won't. At least, we'll try. There's still you to consider."

Pike nodded. "I can still ride out right now."

"No tellin' what Marcy'd do then," McAllister said with a rueful grin. "Besides, there's still the little matter of Ulysses Hungerford, his gunmen, and the future of our lives."

"There is that." He paused. "Look, Charlie, I haven't encouraged her. And I won't. But I also won't treat her cruelly to drive her away. I'm a hard man to be sure, but that doesn't mean I am that way with women. I was raised to treat women with respect, and that's the way I try to act. If I can discourage her without hurtin' her, I'll do so."

"I can't expect anything more, I reckon. So, you'll stay?"

"Long's you let Marcy bring me a piece of pie or cobbler now and again," Pike said with a laugh.

"I let that happen, Viv might just shoot me and you." He chuckled. "But Viv'll talk to Marcy and explain it's okay but to keep a proper distance. I ain't sure it'll do any good, though."

"I'll not encourage her."

"Obliged. Well, guess I should let the other boys back in here."

Pike watched for a moment, then pulled the saddle off the horse.

CHAPTER 19

Marcy was a little more subdued in the morning, but she smiled at Pike even though her mother kept her at arm's length from him as Viv fed him.

"What're you plannin' for the day, Brodie?" McAllister asked as the men ate.

"Do some scoutin', then try'n find my old compadre and see if I can talk to him. Might take a while. Not much else I can do now unless I wanted to just go on down to Hungerford's and challenge all his men to a showdown."

"I reckon that would be a bit foolish," Felder said.

"I'd have to agree." He was surprised when Clay Dunn did not say anything, and he wondered about the bruise on his chin.

"You need someone to go with you?" Felder asked, his voice holding only a modest quiver.

"No. It'd be too dangerous."

"I understand." Relief washed across Felder's face. "I had enough adventure yesterday to last me a while."

Pike finished his meal and went to saddle his horse. Done, he was met outside by Marcy, who handed him a sack with some edibles for his day's travels. He grinned and asked, "You sneak out to do this?"

"No, Mama let me. But I can't linger." She paused as if waiting for him to do something.

But he just said, "Obliged, Marcy." He hung the sack on his saddle horn, mounted up, and rode out.

He spent the next three days scouring the countryside, checking on the young men guarding the cattle, keeping an eye on Hungerford's place, checking on Graystone to see if there were any new arrivals, and looking for Abel Farnum. He did it all with a growing sense of desperation. Time was running short. With no new gunmen showing up in town, Pike figured that Hungerford thought he had enough men to take action soon. He already had, in his usual fashion of small incidents meant to scare the people. His men had burned down Axel Morgan's barn, killed two of Clyde Morgan's horses, and sprayed the Dunn house with bullets, causing no real damage but terrifying Cora Dunn and the others sharing her house these days.

He made cold camps for the most part, eating sparingly of the food Marcy had provided. He did not want to hunt lest he draw attention to himself that would not help.

Just before noon on the third day, he spotted Farnum on the road heading back from Graystone. He quickly swept up over the hill and came down a little way ahead of Farnum, so they would meet face to face.

When Farnum saw Pike coming, he stopped and waited and showed surprise when he saw who it was. "I'll be damned," he said. "What're you doin' in these parts, pard?"

"Could ask you the same, Abel."

"Hirin' out to some folks need help of a kind or another."

"Give up bounty huntin', then?"

"Not entirely. I still do some now and again. Hirin' my gun out is an easier way to make money than spendin' days of ridin' all over the countryside lookin' for desperados who don't want to be found. Pay's better, and the livin' accommodations are a mite better than sleepin' on the ground and eatin' bacon and beans most nights."

"Does sound somewhat appealin'."

"How about we pull off the road here, out of the hot sun, and chat a bit. I got a pint of tanglefoot. We can have a toast to old times."

"Sounds good to me."

They rode into the trees and loosened their cinches to let the horses breathe, then plopped down after Farnum had pulled a small, almost full bottle of whiskey from his saddlebag. He took a healthy swallow, then passed the whiskey to Pike and asked, "You still bounty huntin', Brodie?"

"Yep, for the most part. Took some time off for a spell after I got bullet-punctured bringin' in Jethro Harker and his gang of cutthroats."

Farnum whistled. "That must've taken some doin'. From what I heard, those boys were some bad hombres."

"They were."

"And you did it all by yourself?"

Pike shook his head and took another swig of rotgut. "Had the help of a couple former lawmen. I took the worst of it. Well, all of it on our side. Those two boys managed to drag me back to a town where a sawbones patched me up."

"Sounds like you lucked out."

"Sure did." He handed the bottle back to Farnum, who took a healthy swig, almost emptying it. "Made enough reward money on that one to tide me over for quite a spell, even after splittin' it with the other two fellas." He took the bottle back and drained the little that was left. "So, who'd you hire out to here?"

"Bunch called the Buckskin County Cattlemen's Association."

"Guy named Hungerford hire you?"

"You know him?"

"Know of him. Met him once. Didn't much like him."

"I don't particularly like him either, but as long as he hands me the greenbacks, I'll work for him."

"What're you doin' for him?"

"What you'd expect from a cattlemen's association, riddin' the area of rustlers." He squinted at Pike. "You seem mighty interested in these doins, Brodie. You have some stake in all this?"

Pike hesitated before answering. "A little. Hungerford and his cronies don't really want to get rid of rustlers. They just want to run out a few small-time ranchers so they can take over the land."

"You workin' for 'em?" Farnum asked with a scowl.

"Can't say workin' for 'em, no. Just tryin' to help 'em out a little without any of 'em gettin' killed. I was thinkin' maybe you could be of some help, too."

"I might not be the most upright fella in these parts, but I'm honorable when it comes to stayin' loyal to those who hire me."

"I know that, Abel. I ain't askin' you to leave his employ and help out the small-time folks. Hell, they couldn't pay you anyway."

"So, what're you suggestin'?" His friendliness had disappeared.

Pike was beginning to realize this had been a fool notion. "Maybe give me some idea of what Hungerford and his men're plannin', where and when they're gonna hit."

"Can't do that, Brodie. Like I said, I'm loyal to the man who's payin' me."

"Even if he's in the wrong?"

"That's your thinkin', maybe. I don't know that as a fact. Hungerford and his partners've been losin' cattle, and ain't nobody else around to take 'em except those people you're helpin'. No, can't do what you ask." He pushed himself up, and Pike followed suit.

As they were tightening their cinches, Farnum suddenly spun and punched Pike in the side of the head. Pike staggered and fell to the side. Before he could collect himself, Farnum was on him, pounding him with fists and boots.

Pike tried to cover up as best he could, but he had no chance to fight back. When Farnum backed off for a moment, Pike started to pull a revolver, but Farnum kicked it out of hand, sending it flying a few feet away. Then he went back to hammering Pike again.

Farnum finally let up. Looking down at the groaning Pike, he said, "It ain't bad enough you want me to cross my employer, but you've thrown in with a bunch of rustlers. A man who always said he was on the right side of the law. Hard to figure."

"They ain't rustlers," Pike croaked. "They're honest men and women. It's Hungerford and his partners who're the outlaws here."

"Don't believe that, not one tiny bit, Brodie. Now, I'm gonna let you go. I suggest you ride far and fast away from here. Only reason I don't kill you here and now is because we've been workin' partners now and again in the past. But I'll kill you on sight if you come near me or Hungerford again. And you'll be damned to hell and back if you go back to helpin' those damned rustlers."

Pike said nothing as Farnum picked up Pike's gun in the dirt and emptied the cartridges, tossing them back into the trees. He dropped the pistol on Pike's chest, then pulled his other Colt and did the same with it before mounting his horse. "Mind what I said, Brodie." He rode slowly off.

Pike thought of trying to load one of his pistols and plugging Farnum in the back as he rode away, but he did not have the strength. He lay there a while, testing the pain, moving his arms and legs, checking to see if anything was broken. He decided he was still in one piece, but he would be sore as hell for a while, and maybe not in his finest gunfighting and action form. His anger at Abel Farnum would lessen that pain and the limitations of his movements.

After he finally managed to load his Colts and slide them back into their holsters, he rolled over onto his stomach and awkwardly shoved himself up. He groaned as he did so, but the pain only served to deepen his anger and give him strength. Once he was on his feet, he managed to climb into his saddle. He sat for a few moments to let the world settle down in front of his eyes, then turned for home.

It was nearing dusk when he rode, slumped over the sorrel's neck, into the McAllisters' yard. Viv McAllister, who was feeding the chickens, saw him. "Charlie!"

she shouted. "Connor! Quick!"

The two men, followed by Dunn, Marcy, and a couple of others, ran out and stopped, shocked. Then McAllister said, "Connor, help me get him inside the house. Abe, take Mr. Pike's horse to the barn and tend him."

Viv turned and said, "Marcy, fetch that big pot, fill it with water, and set it on the stove. Go!" She followed the men carrying Pike into the house, where they placed him on the McAllisters' bed. "Looks like you took quite a whuppin'," she said, smiling a little, hoping it would ease his pain a tiny bit.

"I did for certain, Viv."

"Where's it hurt the worst?"

He tried to grin, but it turned into a grimace. "All over," he croaked. More seriously, he said, "Mostly face, head, and ribs. I think a couple of 'em are stove up."

"Ain't much I can do for you, Brodie."

"I know."

"But we'll get you cleaned up and then see what's what."

"Obliged, ma'am."

"Charlie, you and Connor get his shirt off him."

Marcy hurried in with a pot of steaming water and set it down. She rushed out of the room but returned quickly with some

222

cloths, soap, and tincture of iodine. She looked horrified when she saw the bruises covering Pike's face and chest.

chair, weak, and tired of it all. She
walked into the study when she saw the white-
haired Pike enter the drive.

CHAPTER 20

As Pike was saddling his horse in the barn in the morning two days later, Marcy once again brought him a sack with some edibles for his day's travels. He nodded his thanks, though he didn't think he would need it. While he was slinging it over the saddle horn, he saw a slight movement outside, as if someone was spying on him. He wasn't sure, but he thought he knew who it was, and it bothered him — but only a little. There were many more important things to concern himself with. He hung another sack from the saddle horn and tied his thick bedroll behind the cantle.

"Thanks, Marcy," Pike said as he swung into the saddle. He felt considerably better. He still had a little trouble breathing from his cracked ribs, but salve had helped soothe the worst parts of the bruising's pains.

A mounted Charlie McAllister was waiting for him just outside the barn.

"Where're you going?" Pike asked.

"With you."

"No, you ain't. You got no business going where I'm going or doing what I got to do."

"Like hell, Brodie. This is my fight more than yours, and I aim to see it through."

"You're needed here." He glanced at Connor Felder, who passed him on the way to the barn, then looked back at McAllister.

"We take care of business at Hungerford's, there won't be a need for me to be here other than to count our blessin's and get on with life."

"Good chance that if you go with me, you won't be comin' back here, leavin' Viv and all the others here in poor straits."

"I'm comin' along too," Felder said, riding out of the barn.

"Boys, this is not the type of business you're used to. This is my kind of work. You two come along, and I'll have to be concerned you'd do something that'll get us all killed. It'd be a distraction, and that's dangerous."

"Look, I know we ain't gunmen, but we could stage an ambush or something," McAllister said. "There's a dozen gunmen, maybe more. You can't take on all those men by yourself."

"Well, that's for certain. But I ain't exactly

plannin' to go over there and call 'em all out to a gunfight. I may be foolish at times, but I ain't that damn foolish."

"I ain't happy about this," McAllister grumbled.

"You'll be a sight less happy if you go and get yourself killed. And Viv'd be mighty angry, enough to follow you all the way to the gates of hell. Of course, that's as far as she'd get since she wouldn't belong inside, unlike you. The devil'd be afraid to take her, too."

McAllister could not help but chuckle at the vision that conjured. Then his seriousness returned. "You ain't about to change your mind, are ya, Brodie?"

"Nope. And if you're figurin' on tailin' me a little way back, don't. It'll be certain to get us all killed." Pike relented a little. "You're needed here, Charlie. You, too, Connor. These people need you, and you've got to be here to protect 'em if something happens to me."

McAllister winced. "I hadn't thought of that. I figured we'd take care of things out there and our families wouldn't be in danger."

"None of us can guarantee that everything'll be resolved at Hungerford's, and if it ain't, there'll be hell to pay here."

McAllister looked at Felder, who said, "He's right, Charlie. Dependin' on how many of those bastards he removes, if something happens to Brodie, we could be in serious trouble here."

McAllister nodded glumly after a few moments.

"Before you go, Brodie," Felder said, "one other thing bothers me."

"Only one?"

Felder smiled grimly. "Even if you were to kill all of them, includin' Hungerford, which I hope you do, what's to keep Appleyard, Forsythe, and the others from creatin' more trouble for us one day not too far in the future? They're bribin' local, state, and even federal officials, I reckon."

"Nothing, except maybe self-preservation. If they see that you boys've taken down Hungerford and a dozen or more hired gunmen, those left might just decide to look for new ranchland elsewhere. If they want to stay in these parts and try again to run you off, they might just have trouble findin' other gunmen to help 'em out."

"Hope you're right." Felder moved his horse up next to Pike and held out his hand. "Good luck, Brodie."

Pike nodded as they shook.

McAllister took Felder's place. "You've

done so much for us, Brodie. I don't know how to thank you."

"No need for thanks, Charlie. Just take care of Viv and all the others." He rode forward, trying to ignore Marcy, who looked as if she wanted to run to him, and all the others gathered near the barn and in front of the house.

As soon as he was out of sight of the others, he kicked his horse into an easy lope. Before long, he looked back over his shoulder to see someone racing after him. He stopped and turned, waiting. Connor Felder pulled up a few feet from him.

"Thought I told you not to follow me, Connor." His voice was not kind.

"I'm not here to join you but to bring you back. There's trouble at the canyon."

"What?"

"Baldy and Fred went out there to relieve Vin and Willard. They were moseyin' along, in no hurry, which was probably pretty good. They spotted some of Hungerford's men, or at least they thought so. Fred pushed on to warn the others, and Baldy rushed back to the house and told us. I got here as quick as I could."

"Damn. Let's go." Without waiting, Pike slapped the reins on the sorrel's rump, and the animal bolted. Before he reached the

McAllister place, he veered northwest, cutting cross-country across the great meadow beyond the small ranches and on up into the treed-peppered hills leading to the box canyon where the cattle were being kept. As he entered the hills, he cut sharply to the northeast, then began to circle back toward the mouth of the canyon.

Before long he heard gunfire, which filled him with both relief and worry — the former because it meant the young men watching the cattle had not been overcome, the latter because they might be in serious danger.

Pike pushed the sorrel a little harder, and as he neared the canyon's entrance, he spotted Fred Malone, who was hunched over behind a large rock less than forty yards from the opening. "Where's Hungerford's men?" he asked, stopping and startling the young man.

"Last I saw, one of 'em was on the left side, the other two on the right. They almost got in the canyon once, but Vin and Willard drove 'em back." His voice was shaky.

"You haven't thrown in to help your friends?" Pike asked harshly.

"No," he almost whimpered. "I'm scared. Mr. Pike. Plumb scared right down to my socks."

"You got every right to be. Those are some bad men," Pike said harshly. "But those're your friends out there, gettin' shot at, tryin' to protect your and your family's cattle while you sit here hidin'. Well, if you ain't gonna help, stay here out of the way."

Pike rode slowly to the edge of the trees, twenty yards or so from the canyon mouth. He dismounted and pulled his sniper rifle from the special scabbard he'd had made for it some years ago. He'd taken it with him, figuring that if he survived, he would be moving on, and he didn't want to have to return to the McAllister place to get it later.

All three of Hungerford's men, on foot, were easing their way through the trees leading into the canyon. The gunfire from above them had stopped, and Pike wondered whether Vin Mathews and his brother Willard were wounded, dead, or just out of ammunition.

It didn't matter at the moment. Pike lifted the rifle and took aim, and when he fired, one of the gunmen went down. The two others jerked their heads around, searching for where the shot had come from. Pike shoved another cartridge home and fired again, and another man fell. The third started to run, but Pike fired once more, deliberately trying to wound, not kill the man. The man staggered a few steps, then collapsed.

Pike was not certain he had been successful. He put the rifle away, mounted his horse, and cautiously moved forward. The first man was dead, the second was about to breathe his last, and the third had managed to get to his feet, blood running down his pant leg from a bullet hole in his thigh. He was reaching for his revolver when Pike rode up and kicked him in the face, knocking him down. The bounty hunter dismounted, took the man's pistol, and flung it away. He grabbed a leather thong from a saddlebag, hauled the man to his feet, and used the whang to tie his hands. Then he fashioned a quick slip knot in his rope and looped it over the man's head.

"What's your name, boy?" Pike asked.

"None of your business."

"Funny name." Pike mounted his horse. "Come on, None," he said as he moved toward the entrance to the canyon. The man had two choices: walk along as best he could on his wounded leg or strangle to death.

Just inside the mouth of the canyon, Pike yelled, "Vin! Will! It's Brodie Pike. You boys all right?"

"We are," Willard Mathews hollered back.

"Both of us."

Inside the canyon, Willard Mathews came down the left cliff to the floor of the canyon. Vin Mathews started down the other side, but Pike yelled up at him. "Stay where you are, Vin. I'm comin' up." He dismounted, and still tugging "None" along, headed up the sharp trail to the rim, followed by Willard. The outlaw was puffing heavily, and Pike's ribs ached when the two reached the top.

"It's about time you got here," Vin said with a relieved, nervous grin.

"Well, I had some important business to tend to. Haircut and a shave. Had to look my best when I came to rescue you."

"You best get a new barber then," Willard Mathews said with a small, uneasy laugh.

Pike rubbed a hand across his stubbled chin. "Reckon you're right." He grew serious again. "You boys did well, holdin' off this scum."

"Thanks," Vin said. "It wasn't the easiest time I ever had here. Might've been nice if we got some relief a while back."

"Fred and Baldy were on their way to do so when they spotted Hungerford's men. Baldy raced back to McAllister's. Fred stayed behind. I found him hidin' behind a rock out that way a bit."

"I'll have to have a talk with that fella soon's I can," Vin said.

"So what now, Mr. Pike?" Willard Mathews asked.

"Well, first we have a little chat with 'None' here."

"None?"

"Said his name was none of my business. Never heard such a name before, but if that's what he's called, that's what I'll call him."

The two young men snickered.

"Brodie!" Felder yelled from just inside the canyon. "You all right? The boys all right?"

"We're all fine. Go back to the house and see about gettin' these boys some relief."

"Will do, Brodie."

Pike tied the end of the rope holding "None" to a substantial windblown cedar, then shoved the man toward the edge of the cliff and kicked his feet out from under him. The gunman landed with a grunt, and Pike shoved him even closer to the edge. "Now, 'None,' how'd you find out about this place?"

"Don't know."

"Come now, you must know."

"Nope. Mr. Hungerford just told me and the others where to go."

"That I can believe. How many men are with Hungerford?"

"Well, with Buck and Junior crossing the divide," he said, pausing to do some figuring, "fifteen."

"He got more new recruits?" Pike asked, surprised.

"A bunch arrived yesterday. Had trouble catchin' a stage from Denver, they said."

"Damn. Well, all right. Any other people in the house?"

"Don't know why I should tell you anything more. Hell, I'm gonna be dead soon anyway."

"That's for certain. You might want to consider repentin' your wicked past. Don't know as if it'll help much to keep you going to hell, but it might."

"If I went anywhere but hell, I wouldn't know anybody," the man said with a pain-filled laugh.

"Never thought of it that way, but I figure it's true. Still, once I send Hungerford and the others to join you, I'm thinkin' you might not want innocent women or children arrivin' with 'em, though they won't be going there. Still, it'd be shameful for them to have been killed."

"None" was quiet for a bit, then nodded. "You're right about that. I might've done a wagon load of bad things in my time, but I've never killed women and kids. Don't want to be responsible for others doin' so either." He paused as a brief shudder of pain coursed through him. "There's Mrs. Hungerford and their two young'uns, maybe eleven and six. Two maids, a cook, a handyman, and a servant, all of 'em nigras. Hungerford has two men with him as bodyguards all the time."

"Anything else you want to tell me?"

"None" shook his head. "Reckon not. Well, wait. My name is Jim Cleary. If you find someone who wants to put a marker over me, you can tell 'em that."

"I will do so. Any thoughts on your imminent demise?"

"Well, given my druthers, I'd be mighty obliged to postpone it for a spell — maybe twenty, thirty years." He grinned, then sighed. "Reckon that's not gonna come to be. I don't think I'd favor lyin' here bleedin' to death, so unless you're gonna shoot me in the head, I think it'd be best if you tossed me over the cliff. I always figured I was gonna be the honored guest at a necktie party."

Pike nodded. He took the rope from around Cleary's neck and fashioned a proper noose before settling it back into position. "Farewell, Mr. Cleary." He shoved the man over the cliff.

CHAPTER 21

Vin and Willard Mathews looked a little pasty when Pike turned away from the cliff. "You boys all right?" he asked.

Both young men nodded, though the paleness remained. "Yeah," Vin said. "Just that we've never seen anything like that. Seemed a little cold-blooded."

"Not that he didn't deserve it," Willard added.

"You're every bit as hard as Hungerford's men, ain't you, Mr. Pike?" Vin said.

"I can be." He got a faraway look in his eyes, thinking about the trouble he had caused more times than he cared to remember before adding, "I am tryin' to help folks, not run roughshod over 'em."

"Well, you've done right since you threw in with us, Mr. Pike," Willard said.

"It ain't over yet, Will," Pike said with a crooked smile.

"Don't matter. You've already done more

than most folks would do for people like us."

Pike gave one sharp nod. "Well, there's a heap more to be done. Will you boys be all right here for a while longer?" When both nodded, he said, "Good. Hopefully, some relief for you two will be here soon."

"Just as long as it ain't Baldy and that damned Fred," Vin said.

"I'll make sure it ain't, though Baldy was the one who went for help, remember. Don't think too harshly. Wasn't for him, I would've never come to help you two out. I don't reckon you'll have any more trouble, at least for a spell. I figure that eventually, Hungerford'll send out others when he doesn't hear back from these three, but I doubt that'll be very soon."

The Mathews brothers nodded, then Vin chucked his chin toward the taut rope tied to the tree. "What about . . ."

Pike knew he shouldn't say this, but he could not help himself. "Don't want him hangin' around all day?" He laughed.

Both young men looked at him, aghast, then Vin let loose with something that sounded suspiciously like a giggle. Willard snorted, and both burst into laughter.

Pike pulled out his knife, and with a quick slash, cut the rope. Moments later, Cleary's body landed with a dull thud. "You boys have enough food and ammunition?"

"Yep. As long as we get some relief soon."

"You'll have it." Pike headed down off the cliff. At the bottom, he gathered up the end of the rope, mounted the sorrel, rode slowly out, dragging the body. He dropped it near the other two and rode over to where Fred Malone still stood.

"Get on your horse, boy," Pike ordered. He rode on, not much caring whether Malone followed. He did not push the pace, but he did not dawdle either, and before long, he was back at the McAllister place, a subdued Malone in his wake.

"Well?" McAllister asked worriedly as Pike stopped in front of him.

"Will and Vin are fine. They acquitted themselves well. Can't say as much for Fred here. Found him hidin' behind a rock while the other two were protectin' the cattle."

Malone's father, Sylvester, shook his head in embarrassment. "Go take care of your horse, boy. We'll have a talk directly." He took a deep breath, then said, "Sorry, Brodie, Charlie. I never would've thought he'd be a coward. I didn't bring him up that way."

"I know," McAllister said.

"You find someone to take over for Vin

and Will out there, Connor?"

"Was just goin' about it, Brodie."

"I'll go," Arch Blake said. "Soon's I get my horse saddled."

"So will I," volunteered Floyd Dunn, Edgar's son.

The two ran off to the barn.

"How many of Hungerford's men were there?"

"Three."

"None still breathin', I take it," Felder asked.

"Nope."

Abe McAllister moved up to stand next to Pike's sorrel. "I expect you're hungry, Mr. Pike. I expect Mom and," he added with a sly grin, "Marcy will be happy to help. I'll tend to your horse while you're eatin'."

"Obliged, Abe." Pike dismounted and headed toward the house, along with just about everyone else.

Viv and Marcy ladled out a bowl of stew for Pike, and he began eating with gusto. A few minutes later, Floyd Dunn and Arch Blake came in. "We're ready to leave, Mr. Pike."

"Like I told the others out there, I don't expect Hungerford to send anyone else out there too soon. But eventually, he'll realize his men haven't returned and will send a few out to find 'em, so be on your guard at all times. If you look to be outgunned and outnumbered by more than a little, hightail it back here. We'll worry about the cattle later. Make sure you take enough ammunition and food."

"Yes, sir," Dunn said, and he and Blake ran out.

Eager to be on the move, Pike finished his meal quickly. As he was finishing a cup of coffee, Matt McAllister popped into the house. "I hear gunfire from the Dunn place," he said.

"Damn," Charlie McAllister said.

Pike was already moving. His horse still needed rest, so he ran to the corral, cut out a horse, and leaped on. Hoping he could control the horse just with its mane, he raced out, riding bareback.

Charlie and Matt McAllister and Connor Felder were not far behind.

The shooting had ceased by the time Pike pulled the horse to a stop in front of the Dunns' house, which was being shared these days by the Morgan family. The Dunns had moved out of the McAllister place when it became too crowded. He jumped off the horse when he saw Alice Morgan kneeling in front of the house, clutching a child in her arms. The rest of the Dunn and Morgan

241

families stood around in shock.

"They shot her!" Cora Dunn shouted. "They killed that little girl! Just shot her down!"

Pike rested a hand on Alice's shoulder. "We'll get those who did this, ma'am," he said, knowing that such a statement was useless at a time like this. "I swear, I will."

Felder and the two McAllisters sat there on their horses, not knowing what to do. They had seen death before, mostly of adults, though some were youngsters who had died of disease, but they had not experienced the gunning down of a six-year-old girl. All three were numb with shock.

Teeth clenched so hard his jaws ached, Pike mounted the horse and rode back toward the McAllister place. He stopped and put the horse in the corral. Again he blamed himself. If only I hadn't interfered by helping Edgar Dunn, that little girl would be alive, he thought, miserable and disgusted with himself. But the rage would overcome his sadness, at least for a while. Moving deliberately, he marched to the barn and silently saddled his horse.

Felder entered the barn and began saddling his own mount.

"I'm going with you, Brodie, and there's no sayin' no to it this time."

242

"Lookin' to get yourself killed?"

"Nope. Lookin' for revenge."

"You'll get yourself killed."

"No, I won't. I ain't a gunman like you, but I'll do whatever it takes to get back at the men who killed that little girl."

Pike thought that over, then nodded. "Get yourself a weapon and be quick about it."

"You'll wait for me?"

"I will," Pike said tightly.

Felder finished saddling and bridling his horse, then ran to the house. He mostly ignored Becca's worried pleas for him to stay behind until Viv and Charlie McAllister held her still.

When Felder got to the barn, Pike asked, "You got enough cartridges?"

"Yep, and Sam lent me his shotgun and his old Henry. I have plenty of cartridges and shells for them, too."

"Good. Let's ride."

They galloped out, heading east.

"Hungerford's place is the other way," Felder said.

"Yep. But I figured we'd go up this way, make sure Hungerford doesn't have some other child-killin' bastards out here. I doubt it, but I'd rather be sure."

They headed up into the hills but saw no one. Then they swung a little north, and

Pike finally led them on a small trail leading up the hillside toward the spot where he usually surveilled the ranch. They stopped behind a large clump of trees and boulders and tied their horses off, then crept forward until they could check out the ranch. Dusk was not far off.

"What now?" Felder asked.

"We wait."

"For what?"

"To see what they're gonna do. I don't expect them to do much now with night coming on, but I can't be sure. They might think a night raid is a good idea."

Things were quiet for a while, with some men milling about, a few others tending horses, and a few more preparing a couple of carriages, which Pike thought strange. He went and got his spyglass and took a look but didn't see anything out of the ordinary.

Then Felder elbowed him in the ribs and hissed, "Look!"

Three men had come out of the house, one of them looking mighty familiar.

"That's Fred Malone!" Felder gasped. "Ain't it?"

Pike looked through the telescope. "Sure as hell is. Looks mighty chummy with Hungerford's men, too."

"What in the hell?"

"Don't know, but it ain't good." Pike slid the telescope in on itself and stood there thinking, not wanting to let his rage get the better of his sense. Malone and the two gunmen went into the bunkhouse. Soon others began drifting that way, patting the several horses tied to hitching rails outside it as darkness began to sweep over the meadow. He nodded at his silent decision, then spun, went to his horse, and unwrapped his bedroll.

"You ain't plannin' on spendin' the night here, are you?" Felder asked, stunned.

"Of course not. But I need these." He held up three old ax handles.

"What for?"

Pike did not answer. He set the wood aside, rolled up the bedding, and tied it back on the rear of the saddle. Then he pulled a burlap sack off the saddle horn. Opening it, he pulled out a bottle of coal oil wrapped in rags and unwrapped the cloth, then gently put the bottle back in the saddlebag.

"Torches?"

"Yep."

"When did you . . ."

"When you were in the house fetchin' your guns."

"Gonna burn the house down?" Felder seemed both fascinated and worried.

"Nope. Don't want to kill the women and kids in there." His voice caught a little at the last.

"Then, what?"

"You'll see." He wrapped some cloth around each ax handle and tied it in place with a thin rawhide strip. "Let's go." He mounted and moved cautiously to his left, keeping as close to the edge of the trees as he could. With the dark pines behind them, Pike figured he and Felder would not be seen in the dim glow of the half-moon and stars. They stopped facing the rear of the bunkhouse. Pike took some moments to search the area, but he could see no real movement in the dark.

"How're you gonna do this?" Felder asked, his interest piqued.

"With stealth, guts, and a lot of luck." They eased down the slope until they were almost on the flat yet still within the trees. He dismounted, then soaked two rag-covered sticks with coal oil, leaving the third for later if needed.

"I'm gonna make two runs at the bunk-house. Soon as I start my second, I want you to head back up the hill to where you can keep an eye on the front of the bunkhouse. If you get a chance and are willin', shoot whoever comes out of it. Except Malone. I want to capture that son of a bitch if we can."

"Oh, I'm willin' all right," Felder said through a throat constricted with rage at the sight of Alice Morgan kneeling over the body of her slain daughter, Peg.

Pike handed Felder the two torches, then scratched a match to life and lit both. He mounted the sorrel and held out his hand for one torch. With it in hand, he steadied the nervous horse, who pranced a little in fright at having a burning stick so near. Pike kicked the horse into a run, racing across the seventy yards of open space. He pulled to a sharp stop and tossed the torch onto the roof, then galloped back to the trees.

Felder handed him the second torch, and Pike began his second run, while Felder jumped on his horse and bolted up and across the hill. Pike stopped within a couple feet of the bunkhouse and threw the burning switch at a large patch of dried grass along the bunkhouse wall. Then he too sped off.

As he raced toward his former position, he glanced back and saw that flames were beginning to lick their way along the base and roof of the bunkhouse. He stopped, slid off the horse, grabbed his Winchester, and took position behind a boulder. He laid the rifle across the rock and waited. He left the Sharps in its scabbard; it would be too cumbersome for this.

Felder stood nervously a few feet away behind a thick pine, a rarely used old Henry rifle more or less at the ready.

Suddenly men began boiling out of the bunkhouse and running across the meadow. A few grabbed the saddled horses just outside.

"Time to pay up, you sons of bitches," Pike muttered.

Chapter 22

Pike began firing. He hit several men, but how badly they were wounded was uncertain. Hitting running targets was difficult enough, and in darkness lit only by the flickering orange glow of the burning bunkhouse, it was even tougher.

He heard Felder fire and was pleased to see one of the outlaws stumble and fall. Then he saw another of Hungerford's gunmen swing onto a horse. A moment later, he pulled Malone up behind him and headed up the hill to Felder's left.

"You see Malone, Connor?"

"Yep."

"I'm gonna go catch him. You stay here and keep an eye on things. Don't shoot unless you have to. Don't need to call attention to yourself if it ain't necessary now that the bunkhouse is empty and Hungerford's gun hands can look around. But don't hesitate to fire at anyone who seems to be comin' at you or any of those bastards you can take down for sure. I'll be back soon's I can."

"All right," Felder said through a dry mouth. "What if you don't come back?"

"Then you're on your own. Wait as long as you think wise, then head back home. Keep off the main road. Or stay here and kill as many of them as you can." He jumped on his horses and rode out.

Moving through the dark forest was an adventure, but Pike made fairly good progress. He stopped every twenty yards or so and listened. Finally, he heard the sound of a horse moving slowly ahead. He rode as quickly as he dared in the woods until he was at a point where he figured Malone and Hungerford's man would appear. He dismounted, pulled a Colt, and waited.

Within minutes he heard the horse, and when the animal and its two riders were about to pass in front of him, he fired. The bullet slammed into the head of Hungerford's gunman. The horse reared, and Malone rolled off its rump. The gunman slumped to the side as the horse bolted.

Before Malone could rise, Pike hurried forward, wrapped a rope around his torso, and knotted it tight. He hauled the young man to his feet. "Unless that horse comes

250

back, you're gonna have to walk."

"You can't make me."

"True, but I can drag you if you'd like that better." He mounted the sorrel. With the end of the rope in hand, Pike moved off, Malone stumbling along behind him.

It was more than half an hour before Pike could find his way back to where Felder was. As he neared the spot, he called out softly, "Connor, I'm comin' in."

Felder stood. "That's a relief," he said honestly. He spotted Malone as Pike moved forward. "You should've killed that bastard."

"He might have some information we can use. Doubt it, but it's possible. Besides, Sylvester might want that pleasure himself."

"Reckon you're right."

"What's happened here?"

"Everyone took off. Hungerford got in a carriage and rode off in a real hurry, surrounded by what men he had left. I counted eleven."

"No women or children?"

"No," Felder said, surprised. "Did you expect some?"

"One of Hungerford's men I caught out in the canyon said Hungerford had a wife and two kids with him here, as well as some household staff."

Felder shook his head. "Nope, didn't see

any of 'em. Just Hungerford and his men ridin' hell-bent. I reckon they're headin' for Graystone."

"Likely." Pike dismounted and tied Malone to a tree. "Keep an eye on him, Connor."

"Where're you going?"

"Down to the house to see if anyone's there and if they're alive."

"You don't think Hungerford would . . ."

"No, but you never can be sure with a desperate man." He mounted the sorrel and sent it slowly down the hill, letting the animal pick its own way down. On the flat, he found four gunmen dead. To his left, the bunkhouse was now a pile of smoking embers. He warily entered the house and moved down a hallway. In a room halfway down on the right, he heard a slight shuffle. He stopped beside the door and eased it open.

"Don't come no closer, mister," someone said, his voice quaking.

"I ain't here to hurt anyone," Pike said. "I just want to make sure everyone's all right. With Hungerford runnin' off, I was afraid he might've done something wrong here first."

"We all right."

"You the handyman?"

"Yassir."

"When I leave, it'd be smart for you to do something with those bodies outside. Four gunmen are dead. I suggest you dig a hole, toss all of 'em in there, and cover 'em up. They don't deserve any better, and it'll keep the wolves away, maybe. At best, it'll keep a stench from arisin'."

"Are you going to kill my husband?" a woman asked, her voice surprisingly strong.

"Yes."

"He's a good man."

"Maybe to you he is, ma'am. But to others, he's a devilish man, ready to hurt people, even kill 'em to get what he wants."

"He's just protecting his property against rustlers and squatters."

"They ain't squatters. They own their land. And they ain't rustlers. Your husband keeps sayin' they are so he can tell everyone that what he's doin' is right. It ain't."

"You kill him, you'll be leaving these two children without a father."

"That son of a bitch sent a man out to kill a six-year-old girl. I'm gonna kill him, no question, unless his army of scum gets me first. I suggest you and the young'uns get yourself into a carriage and move on."

"No matter. I figure those squatters'll move in here first chance they get. They'll despoil this place, ignorant rustlers that they are."

"I doubt that, ma'am. They're good people, not like the son of a bitch you're married to. Also, if any of them tries to move in here without properly buyin' this place, I'll kill him myself."

"You going to burn down the house like you did the bunkhouse?"

"Nope. I'm gonna ride on out and hunt down your husband and his army of devils. Again, I suggest you get your servants to pack some things in a wagon and drive you and the children to Graystone, or better, some other place where you'll be safe. Graystone ain't likely to be that place."

He did not wait for a response, just headed out and climbed into the saddle. Seeing a saddled horse grazing on the short, sparse grass to his left, he rode over, took the reins, rode across the meadow and up the hill.

"You find the family?"

"Yep. They're all right. Angry but safe." He dismounted and untied Malone from the tree. "Get on the horse, boy."

"No."

"Don't test my patience."

"What're you gonna do, kill me?" It was said with a good dose of fake bravado.

"Nope, but I can do things to you that'll

make you beg me to do so."

Malone blanched. "I can't with me trussed up like this."

"Hold the reins, Connor." Pike bent and grabbed Malone around the knees, then surged up and tossed the young man across the saddle on his belly.

"Hey!" Malone squawked.

"Shut up," Pike said as he mounted his own horse. "Connor, take the reins to his horse and lead the way. Think you can find the trail that leads to the road?"

"Yep." He didn't sound all that certain, but he did, and it didn't take long.

As the three reached the spot where the road eased into the meadow in front of McAllister's house, they slowed and moved cautiously forward. Out in the open, they would be visible in the light provided by the moon and stars.

A voice boomed over the land, "Stop right there, folks!"

"That you, Jules?" Connor shouted. "It's Connor and Brodie."

Pike thought he saw the front door of the darkened house open and shut quickly as a man slipped through, but he was not sure. Just some movement and a slightly moving darker piece of the darkness.

"Move ahead, slowly," the disembodied

voice ordered.

They did so, and when they were fifty yards closer to the house, about twenty-five yards from it, Charlie McAllister's voice came from the front of the house. "What's on that other horse?"

"Fred Malone."

"He dead?" McAllister asked, surprised.

"Nope."

"Then what . . ."

"They got me trussed up like a Christmas goose," Malone said, his voice strained from having ridden on his stomach for an hour or more. "They're gonna tells lies about me and . . ."

"That true?" McAllister interjected.

"Part about him bein' trussed up, yep," Felder said. "The rest, nope."

"Come on ahead then." McAllister opened the house door and said something. Moments later, lanterns sputtered to life inside. Men began drifting over from the barn.

When he dismounted in front of the house, Pike hauled Malone down from the saddle and had to hold him up for a minute since the young man's legs were wobbly. "Get inside," Pike ordered, pushing Malone, who stumbled up the two stairs. In the house, as many people as could fit were packed inside; the others hung around the door. Pike untied Malone and shoved him into a chair.

"What's this all about?" McAllister asked.

It was Felder who answered. "This son of a . . . Fred here is a traitor."

"What?" McAllister snapped.

"We caught him dealin' with Hungerford's bootlickers."

"That ain't true," Malone whined. "They kidnapped me and was gonna torture me." Desperation was thick in his voice.

"Like hell," Pike growled. "You were mighty chummy with those fellas comin' out of the house, and after we started the ruckus, one of those men pulled you up on his horse and lit out."

"He was gonna bring me back to Hungerford."

"Sure he was — so you could give him more information about your people here. With the ruckus, there was no reason to save you unless you were helpful to them. Otherwise, he would have just shot you down."

"Damn you, boy!" Sylvester Malone shouted, leaping forward to get to his son.

"No, Sylvester!" his wife, Sarah, yelled.

Pike stepped in front of the man. "Not now, Mr. Malone. You can have him to do with what you will after we've talked to him some more."

"Why'd you do this, Fred?" McAllister asked through tight lips.

Malone shrugged.

"Wanted to be a big man, did you?" Pike asked sarcastically. "Betray all your family and friends, thinkin' that'd make you a man instead of the worm you are?"

Everyone was trying to take it all in when Will Mathews suddenly burst out, "You told 'em where the cattle was, didn't you, you stinkin' pile of . . ."

"That was why he insisted I come back here for help while he stayed out there," Baldy Morgan snapped. "I should've known something was up, given what a coward you are."

"Darn near got us killed, you skunk," Mathews added. "Wasn't for Mr. Pike, me and Vin would've been dead and all our cattle gone."

"Got anything to say for yourself, boy?" McAllister said.

Malone kept silent, sitting with his head hanging low, hiding his face.

"He's yours now, Sylvester. You can do with him whatever you want except set him free with a horse."

"Let's go, boy," Sylvester Malone said, voice dripping with anger and contempt. He grabbed his son by the neck of his shirt and jerked him to his feet, then half-dragged him outside. Sarah Malone, a pained look on her face, followed.

There was silence in the packed room for some time. Finally, Felder asked, "How'd he manage it?"

Pike shrugged. "Not sure, but I figure that one day when nobody was paying attention, he somehow managed to get to one of Hungerford's men and told them he could tell 'em where the cattle were. It went on from there."

"Damn," McAllister said, then asked, "What're you gonna do now, Brodie?"

"Go after Hungerford, of course. Bring this to an end."

"When do we leave?" Felder asked.

"I'll be leavin' after a spell. My horse needs tendin', and I need some food and a bit of rest."

"I'll be ready."

"No, Connor. You were a big help, but I plan to push hard and go up against almost a dozen gunmen. That ain't your forte, it's mine. Besides, I need you to go out to Hungerford's place and keep an eye on it."

"Why?"

"See if he and his men come back. They do, you haul your rump to Graystone and get me."

"I don't like it."

"Doesn't matter."

Marcy McAllister plunked down cups in front of Pike and Felder, filled them with coffee, and put the pot on the table. She looked at her father, but he shook his head. Moments later, Viv McAllister set a plate of chicken and dumplings before each of the two men. They nodded their thanks and began shoving the food into their mouths.

"Abe'll take care of your horse, Brodie," McAllister said.

"He's already doin' so," Viv tossed in.

"Good boy you got there, Viv," Pike said, winning a nod and a warm smile from the woman.

"You can stay the night here. No need to be sleepin' out in the barn with the others. You'll have to share space with Connor, though."

Pike nodded.

Chapter 23

The sky was just beginning to lighten when Pike swung into the saddle. He felt considerably better. The meal last night and a hearty breakfast minutes ago, along with a good though short night's sleep, had him feeling pretty good. Even the pain from his beating had lessened considerably.

He and Felder rode out together, but not far down the road, Felder asked, "You sure you don't want me along?"

"Yep. It ain't likely Hungerford'll come back here anytime soon, but if he does, I want someone here I can trust."

Felder nodded, not happy. Minutes later, just as Felder was going to turn onto the trail toward the Hungerford ranch, the two men heard a scream from behind them.

Both turned and raced down the road, sliding to a stop when they saw Clay Dunn pull Marcy McAllister off her horse. He slapped the struggling young woman, then slapped her a second time. She screamed again.

"Clay!" Felder yelled. "Stop it, Clay!"

The young man turned wild eyes on Pike and Felder. "She ain't your woman, Pike," he yelled.

Felder moved closer. "What in hell's gotten into you, Clay?"

"I'm gonna marry Marcy, but Pike was tryin' to steal her away from me."

"Like hell," Pike snapped. "Now, leave her be."

"You ain't gonna tell me what to do no more, you bastard." He ungracefully pulled a gun from his belt.

"No!" Felder shouted.

"Don't do it, boy," Pike warned.

Dunn did not listen. He began to bring the pistol up toward Pike.

"No, Clay," Felder pleaded. "Don't . . ."

Pike waited as long as he could, hoping Dunn would come to his senses, but the young man kept lifting the pistol. With a sad shake of his head, Pike pulled a Colt and shot Dunn in the chest.

Marcy screamed, Felder groaned, and Pike sighed.

Felder dismounted and went to Marcy. He took the screaming, crying girl in his arms and tried to calm her.

When she had regained some of her composure, Felder released her and held her at arm's length. "What was this all about, Marcy?"

Still sobbing, she said, "I wanted to catch Brodie and say goodbye to him if he wouldn't take me with him. I knew he wouldn't be coming back here however things worked out. Clay followed me, sayin' he loved me and wanted me to marry him. I told him no, and he dragged me off my horse. I tried to stop him, but he slapped me once, then again."

Felder looked at Pike. "This make any sense to you, Brodie?"

"Some, I reckon. I never encouraged her, but she seems to think she's in love with me. As for Clay, I caught him snoopin' around a couple of times when Marcy brought me sweets of an evening."

Felder shook his head. There was no good to come from this, he figured. "Get on your horse, Marcy." When she did, Felder lifted Dunn's limp body and tossed it across his saddle. He mounted his own horse. "Go on ahead with your business, Brodie. I'll take these two back to Charlie's and explain it to him."

"I can go with you and deal with whatever Charlie thinks is best."

263

Felder smiled a little. "What you're gonna do in Graystone is your business, you said. It's what you do. This is my business — family business. Go on, get."

"You sure?"

"Yep."

Pike turned and headed back down the road.

He pushed hard, and when he reached Graystone before noon, he stopped in front of the Cattlemen's Association club and dismounted. Taking a deep breath, he went inside. The place was empty except for the bartender. "Where's Hungerford?" he asked.

"Not here."

Pike drew his revolver and fired. The bullet passed within an inch of the bartender's head and shattered some bottles behind him. "Where's Hungerford?"

"Went to Mr. Appleyard's," the bartender answered nervously.

"His men?"

"Gone with him."

"Appleyard's place is the one not too far southeast of here?"

"Yes."

Pike spun, climbed into the saddle, and whipped the sorrel into a run. He slowed once he left town, not wanting to punish the horse, but he kept up a good pace. Right around noon, he arrived and rode straight up to the house. One of the two gunmen he had seen during his surveillance the other day was sitting on the porch, puffing on a hand-rolled cigarette. "Howdy," Pike said.

"What d'you want here?" the gunman asked.

"A little politeness might be a good start."

"Hell," the man drawled, "either state your business or get the hell off Mr. Appleyard's ranch."

"I'm here to see the boss."

"I'm the boss."

"You're a mouse turd. I want to speak to Appleyard."

The man looked as if he were about to draw on Pike but thought better of it. "Why?"

"Lookin' for a job."

"We got enough cowpunchers."

"Do I look like I'm a cowpuncher?"

"Reckon not." He grinned somewhat unkindly. "But you do look like you been stampeded over by a herd."

"Reckon I do. Take me to your boss."

"Just wait here. I'll see if he wants to talk to you." He headed inside.

Pike dismounted, then marched up the

steps to the porch and through the door.

"You'll have to wait outside," a woman said.

Pike looked at her. She was a short, slightly plump, busty woman with a pale face and long red hair streaked with gray. "And you are?"

"Bernice. The maid for Mr. and Mrs. Appleyard."

"How many other gunmen are here?"

"Countin' you?"

Pike grinned. "I'm on the good side."

Bernice cocked her head at him, then smiled. "Just one. Josh something. He's in the kitchen, havin' coffee and likely annoying Collette, the cook."

"Who else is in the house?"

"Samuel, a black chap does odd jobs and chores 'round the place, and Slim. He's Mr. Appleyard's manservant."

"Mrs. Appleyard?"

"She's upstairs with the youngsters."

"You get along with her?"

"About as well as any maid and her mistress."

"She trust you?"

"Reckon she does. Again, about as much as a mistress will trust her maid."

"What's the name of the one I spoke to outside?"

"Earl. Why do you want to know all this?"

"Because when Earl comes out of Apple-yard's office there, he's gonna call Josh." Bernice cocked an eyebrow at him again and he grinned, but there was little humor in it. "When that happens, I want you to get Mrs. Appleyard, the children, Collette, Samuel and Slim — and you, of course — somewhere safe in the house. There might be trouble, and I'd rather you folks not get hurt."

"You gonna teach them boys some manners?" Bernice asked hopefully.

"Better. I aim to send them packin'."

"Be a blessing."

"What're you doin' here, woman?" Earl demanded as he stomped up.

"Just keeping our visitor from getting bored."

"Go back to work."

"Yes, sir." She moved off, tossing an angry glance at Earl over her shoulder.

"Mr. Appleyard says to tell you to go to hell, mister."

"That's mighty rude of him." Before Earl could say anything, Pike popped him hard in the nose and swiftly reached out and jerked Earl's Colt from his holster. "Now, call your friend Josh out here."

"If I don't?"

Pike popped him in the snout again, this time breaking his nose. "It'll get worse for you from here."

"Josh!" Earl shouted. "Come on out here. Boss wants to see us."

A tall, gangly young man came out of the kitchen and started down the hallway. He looked like he'd just had some fun, likely at the expense of Collette, Pike figured. When he was a few feet away, he asked, "Hey, Earl, who's this saddle tramp?"

Pike stepped around Earl, who was still holding his bloody nose, and whacked Josh on the head with the barrel of Earl's pistol.

Josh reeled, and Pike snatched Josh's pistol as well.

"Both of you take off your gun belts." When they did, he holstered their revolvers and slung the belts over his shoulder. "Now, let's go have a wee chat with Appleyard."

Pike pushed the two disarmed gunmen into the office, where a stout, well-dressed, bewhiskered man sat behind a large oak desk.

"What's the meaning of this?" Appleyard roared. "I thought I told you . . ." He spotted Pike. "Who the hell are you?"

"Name's Brodie Pike."

Appleyard looked from Earl to Josh, then

back. "I thought I told you to get rid of this bum?"

"He tried," Pike said. "But if you're gonna hire hands to handle your dirty work, you need to hire better ones than these two."

"Like you?"

"Yep. If I were interested."

"You aren't?"

"Nope."

"Then why are you here? Earl said you wanted to talk to me about a job."

"I just told him that to get in to see you. When that didn't work, I took other measures."

"All right, so what is it you want?"

"Where's Hungerford?"

"How the hell should I know?"

"He was headed here this mornin'." Pike had the smallest twinge of doubt about whether the bartender had lied to him, but it faded almost as quickly as it came.

"Whoever told you that was lyin'."

"You're a lyin' sack of goat turds. Where is he?"

"I see no need to answer that. You'll be dead before the day is out."

"How will you accomplish that? These two are no help to you, and Hungerford's gun hands are with him, wherever he is. It's too far to get them here soon anyway, I expect."

"Oh, I can reach them all right. I'll have one of my ranch hands ride over there right away."

"So, you do know where he is." Pike grinned harshly. "Besides, it'll take most of the day just to find a ranch hand on this spread, much longer if you do it yourself since I would wager than you've never been out on the ranch with the hired hands. And you got no one else to send."

"I'll have my manservant do it."

"Doubt it. He's with the other servants, and I think your wife, too, hidin' out somewhere in the house."

"Why you insufferable . . ."

"Shut your cakehole, Appleyard. Your days of trying to run innocent, hard-workin' simple folk off their land are over. Your days of hirin' child killers are over too." A bit of his rage entered his voice.

"Like hell. It'll be a cold day in Hades before I let some saddle bum like you tell me what I can or can't do." He started to reach inside a desk drawer.

"Don't," Pike warned. When Appleyard did not stop, Pike pulled a six-gun and shot him through the right shoulder.

"You shot me!" the rancher said, stunned, then blanched as shock hit him.

"Indeed I did, and I'll do so again if you

annoy me further. Now, I don't care if you stay on this ranch, sell it, or give it away, but you will leave those small ranchers alone. If you don't, I will come back here and put a bullet through that pumpkin on your shoulders. Is that understood?"

"Yes," Appleyard muttered as the pain of his wound intensified.

"Good. Now, where's Hungerford?"

"He was headin' to Granville's, then back to Graystone. Said he wanted to be back there before dark."

Pike nodded and looked at the two former bodyguards. "He owe you anything?"

"Ain't been paid for the week," Josh said.

"He carry money on him?"

"Yep. Wallet in an inner jacket pocket."

"Get it. Do not try anything foolish."

"I won't." Josh walked over to where Appleyard was sweating with agony, opened the man's coat, and retrieved a leather billfold.

"Take what you and Earl are owed, and maybe a fin each for your troubles." When Josh hesitated, Pike added, "No, you can't keep it all. He's a scoundrel all right, but you boys ain't much better, and you don't deserve any more than what you're owed."

Josh took the amount, then dropped the wallet on the desk. "So, what about me and

Earl?" he asked. "I don't think you're plannin' to shoot us. If you were, you wouldn't have had me get our wages."

"What you and Earl are gonna do is ride fast and hard away from here. And not come back. That would be most unhealthy for you."

"You broke my nose, damn you," Earl said. "I might come gunnin' for you."

"Sure, I broke your nose. I could've shot you down right off. Still can if I get any more lip from you."

"He's right, Earl," Josh said. "I thought this'd be kind of a lark. Protect this fat cat and strut through Graystone, havin' people look at us in fear, even though we didn't do much real gun work. I think this fella's right. Buckskin County is gonna be a mighty dangerous place real soon. I'd much rather be somewhere far away when that happens."

Earl hesitated only a moment before nodding. "See ya, mister," he said, turning for the door.

"Not so fast, Earl. You and Josh can wait a bit longer. Bernice!" he bellowed. "Come on down here to Appleyard's office."

A minute later, the maid popped into the room and stopped. Her pasty face grew even paler when she saw the blood from Appleyard's wound.

"He's hurt, but he'll live if someone gets a doctor here soon. Have Slim ride to Graystone to get a doctor. Tell him that if he goes anywhere but to Graystone to get a doctor, I'll hear about it, and he will not be happy when I visit him." The last part was a lie, considering there was no way he would be able to learn of it, but Bernice got the point.

"He'll do what you say."

"Good." He turned to the two former gunmen. "All right, boys, we'll head out to the barn, where you'll saddle your horses — after you hand over your Winchesters and your saddlebags so I can check those for any other firearms you might have. Then we'll ride out a ways, and you'll get your guns back. Unloaded, of course."

Things went smoothly, and three miles outside of town, Pike tossed each man his weapons and gun belt. "I'll tell you again. Ride west and keep goin', and don't think about comin' after me. You'll end up on the wrong side of the grass." He turned his horse and galloped off.

When he hit the trees at the far end of the meadow, he stopped and waited, watching his back trail. He wasn't sure, but he figured Earl might come after him. The young man had been humiliated, and he didn't seem the kind to take that lightly.

It was not long before Earl came riding hard toward him. As Earl entered the trees, Pike said, "Stop!"

Earl jerked his horse to a halt, looking around frantically for Pike. The latter came out from behind a stout pine, Colt in hand. "I told you not to come after me, boy. You're a damn fool for not listenin'."

"You ain't gonna give me a chance?" Earl asked, fear reaching deep inside of him.

"That would make me a damn fool." With little emotion, he shot the would-be gunman through the heart. He lifted the body from where it had fallen off the horse and tossed it across the saddle, then tied it down, though not all that tightly. He turned the horse to face the meadow and gave it a sharp smack on the rump to send it racing away.

"Maybe Josh'll give you a fitting burial. Or maybe not." He climbed into the saddle and set off at a fast pace.

CHAPTER 24

Pike pushed hard toward Granville Forsythe's ranch. As he rode, he wondered whether it would be better to find Hungerford there or in Graystone. Either place would put the odds heavily in Hungerford's favor, but he realized that if Hungerford and his men were at Forsythe's, he did not have to confront him there. He could ride on and find a spot on the road back to Graystone where he could set an ambush. There should be places where the aspen- and pine-covered hills would provide just such a place.

That choice became moot when he sat at a short distance and surveyed the place with his spyglass. He saw no sign of Hungerford and his men, and there was no place almost a dozen gunmen could be sequestered. He didn't see Hungerford's carriage either if he had even brought it. If he had, he likely would've left it right outside the house if he planned to go back to Graystone by evening.

He put the telescope away and vowed, "I'll be back for another visit, Forsythe, and you won't like it." He was about to pull himself into the saddle when he shook his head in annoyance. The sorrel had been hard-used already. He loosened the cinch to let the animal breathe, then allowed it to graze on the thick grass amid the trees.

As he waited, he saw a chubby well-dressed man come out on the porch, flanked by two gunmen. He smiled grimly, pulled the sniper rifle from the scabbard, and stuck several extra charges in his shirt pocket, then knelt and took aim through the scope. He fired, and the man he assumed was Forsythe went down. He ejected the shell and slid another home. Both gunmen were kneeling next to their boss. Pike took aim again and fired at a much smaller target. One gunman's head exploded when the .52-caliber bullet struck it. He swiftly rechambered and waited a moment until the other gunman stood. The man took one look around, then turned to head into the house. Pike fired, hitting the man in the back. The bounty hunter smiled with satisfaction.

He forced himself to wait for half an hour before tightening the cinch again. As he mounted, he patted the horse's neck.

"Sorry, old fella, but we got some more hard ridin' ahead of us. If I live through this, I'll treat you especially well soon's I can."

He pushed hard again, the sorrel loping along strongly and unfailingly. Trees began lining the road as they pressed ahead, growing thicker and spreading far to either side. As he neared a spot where the road wove between two hills that rose for the next mile, Pike pulled to a stop. He could see a cloud of dust ahead. Quickly he grabbed his telescope and peered through. "Well, lookee there," he muttered. "It's them." They appeared to be just moseying along.

Putting the spyglass away, Pike turned the horse to the left and kicked it into a gallop. Before long, he swung northwest into the mountains. He pushed the sorrel hard, muttering, "Sorry, horse. I know I'm askin' a lot of you, but it's gotta be done."

They loped through a narrow gap where a rock had been split by some powerful force, and they were at the top of the mountain. He rode down the other side, then up again as an even taller hill rose before him. Just over the top of that one, Pike stopped. He had a good view of the road as it meandered through the trees between the hills, so he tied the horse to a bush and crept forward, Winchester in hand. He left the Sharps in its scabbard since the single-shot breech-loading rifle would not be good for the rapid fire rate he would need and took up a position in a spot just wide enough to accommodate him between a thick spruce and a rough boulder.

The group finally appeared, and Pike tried to draw a bead on Hungerford, but with gunmen all around the rancher and the bouncing of the carriage, it was difficult. He quickly turned his attention to the hired men. He didn't much care which ones he took out — except Abel Farnum, who was on the far side of the carriage to the rear. Pike wanted Farnum to suffer.

He sighted on one of the men at the front and put a .44-40 slug in his chest. The horse bolted, the dead man flopping wildly as it ran. Other horses reared or danced nervously, their riders trying to control them. The men in front charged ahead, as Hungerford whipped the horse pulling the carriage and raced down the road.

Pike fired several more times, missing more than he hit, but three more men went down. One of the others suddenly pointed in his direction, having seen the gun smoke. Several fired up at him with their pistols, but the range was a bit too long for accuracy when the men were firing from horseback.

Pike lingered a few moments longer, then scooted away from his position, mounted his horse, and rode deeper into the trees. He didn't think anyone would come looking for him. They'd be hightailing it to Graystone, he figured.

He waited about twenty minutes, reloading his Winchester while he sat there, before heading down to the road. Two of the three men lying there were dead, and the third was close to it. Pike relieved that one of his weapons right off, then got the others' gun belts and holstered their six-guns. He might find uses for them, he thought.

He mounted the sorrel and headed up the road, in no rush. Half a mile away, he spotted the first man he had shot. The corpse was lying on the side of the road, but his horse was nowhere around. "Well, that evens the odds a bit," he announced to the wind and birds.

Slowing as he neared the town, he wondered how to handle things. Probably Hungerford and most if not all of his remaining men were at the Cattlemen's Association club. He considered setting the building on fire but discarded that idea since innocents might get killed if the fire spread to other buildings, which it likely would. Finally, he decided he would wait till the morrow. He'd get some rest and let them think he might have moved on.

He headed to his frequently used spot on the hill west of town and let the horse drink from the small pool, then hobbled it and allowed it to graze. He rested for a while, wishing he had coffee and food before he dozed. When he awoke, it was dark, and he was hungry. "Damn," he mumbled.

He unhobbled the horse and rode down to the town, sticking to the rear of the nearest buildings. A little way past the cribs behind one of the saloons, he tied the horse to the loose board of a building and moved up the alley between that building and the saloon. He stopped in the shadows before he reached the street, which was lit by a series of tall lanterns, and stood there considering his options, none of them good.

As he was debating whether to move into the street and try to buy some food at a restaurant, a man came out of the saloon on his left and headed toward him. The man hopped off the boardwalk and took two steps toward the one on the other side when Pike said, "What the hell're you doin' here, Connor?"

Felder stopped and was about to face Pike, but the latter said, "Don't turn. Go up the steps and lean against the wall."

When Felder has done so, Pike said, "I asked what're you doin' here."

"Lookin' for you."

"Why?" Pike was suspicious.

"It was obvious nothin' was happening at Hungerford's, so this afternoon I headed here."

"What happened at Charlie's?"

"He was not pleased, I can tell you that. He was angry at Clay and you and Marcy. I think she's gonna be watched mighty closely for a while, at least. He was sad about Clay, but that turned to anger when I explained what had happened. I also explained to him that you did not lead Marcy on. He was skeptical at first since you and he had some words over her."

"We did, and I told him then I had no designs on her."

"That's what he said. Anyway, he accepted it for what it was: a flighty girl, a hotheaded young beau, and a reluctant gunman."

"Reluctant?"

"You didn't want to give Marcy any encouragement, and you sure as hell didn't want to shoot Clay. So, once that was cleared up, I headed to Hungerford's. Like I said, nothing was goin' on there, so I came here. I was wonderin' where to look for you since Hungerford didn't seem to be here, at

281

least 'til almost dark."

"Where is he?"

"Cattlemen's Association club, as you probably thought. Some of his gunmen have been prowlin' the town. Don't know why, though."

"Lookin' for me, I reckon. I took out four of 'em this afternoon." He paused. "If you really want to help, go get me some food."

"Where should I bring it?"

"Alley between the hardware and the bank."

"I'm sensin' you don't trust me." He sounded almost hurt.

"After Malone, I have doubts about everyone. Except me."

"Guess that makes sense. I am on your side, though."

"I reckon you are, but I got to be cautious. Be careful of anybody watchin' you when you bring me something to eat. Don't need pryin' eyes."

"Right."

When Felder headed off, Pike went and moved his horse, then wandered up another alley, keeping a watch on the street. Twice he saw a Hungerford man wander by on the other side of the main street and had to fight the impulse to shoot them down. Finally, he saw Felder returning from a restaurant carrying a napkin-covered plate and what seemed to be a jar. He waited a bit longer before he headed to the assigned meeting place.

Felder was waiting. When he saw Pike, he said, "I thought maybe you'd gone back to wherever it is you're stayin'."

"Soon. Come on." He walked to the far end of the alley and got his horse, then moved on foot across the refuse-coated patch of dirt and to where the stream ran sluggishly and sat on a recently fallen log. "What do you have for me?"

Felder handed him the plate. "This late, I couldn't get much. A few hard eggs and a couple slices of ham with bread." He grinned a little. "And a pickle."

"What's in the jar?"

"Coffee. Figured you could use some."

"Good thinkin'. Have you tried it?"

Felder was taken aback. "Think I'm tryin' to poison you?"

"Nope. Just wonderin' how good — or bad — it tastes."

Felder shrugged and unscrewed the cap, then took a large swig. He winced. "It's awful."

"Not Becca's, eh? Or Viv's?"

"Hell, no." He handed the jar to Pike, who drank deeply.

"Yep, pretty bad. Almost as bad as what I make when I'm on the trail." He drank some more, then ate with gusto. After he finished with the food, he polished off the coffee. "Time for you to get yourself a room unless you're plannin' on ridin' back to McAllister's tonight."

"Nope. Got a room set up. What about you?"

"I'll be bunkin' out there." He jerked his head toward the hill.

Felder nodded and left. Pike headed back to the alley and kept watch. His vigilance paid off soon when he saw Farnum walking down the street toward him. He grinned viciously and eased out a pistol. As Farnum went to cross the alley, Pike whacked him hard across the head with his pistol barrel. He managed to catch the man before he fell and dragged him back into the alley.

He gave Farnum a minute to regain most of his equilibrium, then shoved him ahead. Farnum groggily stumbled forward. At the end of the alley, Pike pushed his former friend out into the dim moon- and starlight, then slammed him against the wall. Pike slapped him a couple of times, trying to get him to focus. When he did, his eyes widened. "Pike? I thought you were long gone from these parts."

"Reckon you thought wrong. And you made a big mistake." He pulled the bandanna from around Farnum's neck and shoved it in the man's mouth. Before Farnum could react, Pike hauled off and slammed his bootheel with all the force he could muster against Farnum's shin. The tibia snapped, and Farnum's eyes bulged with the shock and pain.

Pike let him slip down to a knee, then stepped back and began pummeling him with fists and boots. Breathing heavily, he finally stopped, realizing Farnum was unconscious or near to it. "I won't be as big a fool as you were." He plunged his knife into Farnum's chest.

After wiping the knife off on the man's shirt, Pike headed back up the alley. Just outside it and to his right was his horse. Pike grabbed the rope hanging from the saddle and went back to where he had left Farnum. Pike looped the rope around his neck, then mounted his horse. With the rope dragging Farnum in the dirt, the bounty hunter rode down the alley. There were few people out at this hour. Pike moved into the street and turned left, then kicked the sorrel into a run. As he reached the front of the Cattlemen's Association building, he let go of the rope. Farnum's body rolled to a stop.

Pike did not slow but charged out of town, turned onto the road, then soon after, headed into the trees up the hill. He figured he would be safe at his usual spot.

CHAPTER 25

Pike rode boldly into Graystone the next morning, stopped in front of the Cattlemen's Association club, dismounted, and tied his horse to the hitching rail. He had his Colts in place, and around his neck were two gun belts taken from the Hungerford men he had killed the day before as makeshift shoulder holsters. Tucked into his belt at the small of his back was Jethro Harker's specially made Colt. It was a different caliber than his own and those of Hungerford's men, but it would be a comfortable backup, he thought.

People stopped their activities to look at him. An excited buzz filtered through the town.

The door opened and one of Hungerford's men stepped out, then a second. They moved a few feet apart on the boardwalk. "You want something here?" one of the men asked.

Pike said nothing, just stood there waiting.

"He's so scared he can't even talk, Lou."

"That true?" Lou asked, a sneer on his face.

Pike shook his head. "I'm just waitin' till you boys finish up your comedy act here."

"Why, you son of a bitch," Lou snapped, yanking out his pistol.

He was not fast enough. Pike calmly snatched out one of his Colts and fired twice, hitting Lou in the chest with both shots. Then Pike swung toward Lou's partner, and in an instant, put two bullets in that man's chest too.

"That's enough gunplay from you," a voice behind Pike said. "Drop your weapons and come along nicely."

Pike looked over his shoulder to see Marshal Haney pointing a six-gun at him, a smug look on his face. He prepared to whirl and shoot Haney, figuring he was good enough to get the lawman before Haney got him. Then he heard a thump behind him and looked over his shoulder again.

Connor Felder stood behind a wavering Haney, shotgun in hand, having just pounded the marshal's head with the butt.

"Obliged." He looked forward again, keeping an eye on the open door. He saw no activity.

"Least I could do." He hesitated for a moment, then asked in a slightly unsteady voice, "Should I shoot him?"

Pike wasn't sure Felder could do it if he asked him to, but Pike shook his head. "Not unless he aims to cause more trouble."

Pike stepped onto the wooden sidewalk and picked up Lou's revolver. He suddenly tossed it inside, then turned, flattening his back against the wall next to the door. There was no reaction from inside, and he began to sweat. He knew they were waiting for him; what he didn't know was where they were. He reloaded his Colt.

People were edging closer, and Pike shook his head at the foolishness of it, but he said nothing. It was their folly, not his. "Connor, thump Haney again and put him out of commission. Take his gun and shove it in your pocket or something, then come up here next to me." But with his hand, he indicated the wall on the other side of the door.

It took a few moments for Felder to understand, then he nodded. He pounded Haney's head with the scattergun's butt again, and the marshal collapsed. Felder picked up the lawman's pistol, stuck it in a coat pocket, and headed to where Pike had directed him, moving cautiously.

Pike kept alternating his attention between keeping an eye on the door and sweeping the crowd to make sure no one there posed a threat.

"Poke that scattergun through the door," Pike whispered, hoping Felder, but no one else could hear him. "When I say so, let go with both barrels."

Felder nodded and eased the shotgun's muzzle around the doorjamb. Pike nodded. Felder fired into the room, and the bounty hunter dashed through the door, keeping low and rolling toward the right side.

Pike flipped over one of the thick tables and crouched behind it for protection. He peered around one side but could see nothing. "Damn." He didn't know what he had expected, but he cursed himself for not having thought of the fact that the men could be anywhere, including upstairs. What the hell am I gonna do now? he mused, but he had no answer.

Suddenly a gunshot shattered the window and the glass mirror behind the bar. Another shot came, and Pike scuttled away from his table to take refuge behind one of the club's thickly upholstered chairs. He peered out as more shots came from outside. In the splintered mirror, he could see the reflections of two men. That left three men with Hungerford, which didn't help any as long as the two gunmen were safely hidden behind the bar.

More gunfire, slow but steady, came through the window, and Pike decided he had to take a chance. Bent over, he ran to the side of the bar nearest the wall holding the front door. As a seventh, then an eighth shot rang out, he rose, moved the last two feet to see behind the bar, and opened fire. He emptied one Colt, then grabbed one of the pistols from a dead gunman's gun belt and fired some more.

He felt a bullet crease his neck and another the ribs on his right side, and a third on the upper arm, then suddenly there was silence. Pike stepped forward. Both men had been hit more than once and were covered with blood. One was dead, the other close to it. Pike knelt by his side and started to reload his six-guns. "Where's Hungerford?" he asked.

"Don't know," the man gasped.

"You owe him any loyalty?"

"No."

"Then tell me where he is."

"Upstairs. Room Six. At least, that's where he went. Don't know if he's still there."

"The other three of you skunk-eaters with him?"

"Yeah. Maybe not in the same room, though."

"Obliged. May you rest . . ." The man was dead. Pike closed the corpse's eyes and stayed where he was, scanning the upper floor. There were eight rooms on the second floor; Hungerford could be in any of them, and his men in a different one or several.

"Damn, this ain't getting me nowhere." He took a deep breath. "Hell with it, Brodie. Time to end it." He rose, strode across the floor, and headed up the stairs as quietly as he could. At the top, he paused. The second floor was laid out in a U shape, with two rooms on one short side to his left, four rooms along the rear wall, and two on the other wall. He swung to his left and went to Room 1. He listened intently but heard nothing, then gently tried the knob, which turned easily. He flung the door open but stayed to the side. Nothing happened, so he peeked around the doorjamb, but there was no one inside.

He moved on to the next one, but for some reason, he decided to skip it. He paused to the side of the door to No. 3, went to reach for the doorknob, and noticed a shadow moving across the floor under the door as if someone had walked in front of the window. He nodded. The door opened easily, and he shoved it open, then spun inside. The gunman there was startled, which gave Pike enough time to shoot him twice, once in the chest, once in the head as the man fell.

"Two more," Pike muttered, wiping the sweat off his face with a sleeve.

A bullet thudded into the wall well away from him, coming from an angle that would have made it nearly impossible to hit him. Pike crouched and looked cautiously out. Judging by the angle, the projectile had come from Room 7. "You made yourself a fatal mistake, boy," Pike said quietly as he moved out of the room and swiftly down the hall to No. 7. As before, he stopped just to the side of the door. He supposed the man didn't know that Pike had figured out where the shot had come from. Pike slid his own Colt into a holster, pulled one of the extra Colts, and emptied it through the door. A thud came from inside, which gave Pike half a moment of satisfaction, but he was still cautious.

He took out the other extra Colt, thumbed back the hammer, took a deep breath, and kicked in the door, spinning to the side as he did. The man was dead, at least two of the six shots Pike had fired having hit him.

"Your turn, Hungerford," Pike said. He reloaded both Colts plus his own, then stepped out into the hallway. He was fairly certain Hungerford would not box himself in by staying in a room on the short sides. That meant he was likely in 4, 5, or 6 since he had already checked No. 3. He thought 6 might be the right one, not only because the dying gunman downstairs had said so, but because it seemed the most likely. Rooms 4 and 5 were almost directly ahead when coming up the stairs. Rooms 3 and 6 were in the corners, offering protection but not being boxed in.

"Well, let's go find out." He walked quietly up to room 6 and waited to the side of the door again. He watched the floor, hoping to see a shadow move, but there was none. Then he heard a low cough and smiled grimly. He tried the doorknob, which turned without trouble, so he turned it all the way and shoved the door open but stayed to the side. Then he tossed his hat across the room. It was enough of a distraction that he swept inside and fired three times at the gunman, killing him, but he took a bullet in the fleshy meat just above his hip. He gasped. Not again, he thought.

He pushed the thought out of his mind as

he stared at Hungerford, who was en-sconced in a plush chair. "Looks like your end has finally come, Mr. Hungerford." He returned his revolver to its holster and pulled Harker's fancy Colt. He figured this was a somewhat special occasion and de-served a rather special weapon.

"You're not going to shoot me in cold blood, are you?" Hungerford squeaked.

"Don't see why I shouldn't, but if it'll make you feel better, you can pick up your hireling's pistol and take me on. I am wounded, as you can see."

Hungerford's face was pasty and covered with sweat. He hesitated, then gingerly reached for the gunman's revolver and snatched it up. He didn't get it more than six inches off the floor when Pike put a .45-caliber bullet in that arm. He then calmly shot Hungerford in the left knee, eliciting a screech of pain and terror.

"Sending men to kill children is not the action of a good man."

"I didn't tell anyone to do that," Hunger-ford gasped. "I just wanted him to send some bullets flying to scare those people."

"Either you're a lyin' sack of skunk drop-pings, or you hired men too stupid to understand orders." Pike shot Hungerford again, this time in the right shin.

"Stop!" Hungerford screamed. "Please!"

"Oh, I don't think you've quite suffered enough, Mr. Hungerford." He shot the man in the left shoulder.

Hungerford was crying now and whimpering in pain.

Pike decided he had had enough. "Goodbye, you scabrous piece of donkey shit." He calmly fired a bullet into Hungerford's head.

Pike returned the .45 Colt to his belt, then pulled one of his .44s, just to be on the safe side. He felt the pain of his wounds, but even more, he felt sad that things had come to this — that there were men in the world like Ulysses Hungerford who caused so much pain. He shrugged it off. Such men were plentiful.

He went downstairs and outside. The crowd had grown, and most of the people gaped when Pike walked out. Felder offered a big grin of relief.

"You the one shootin' through the window, Connor?"

"I was." He seemed rather proud.

"Obliged. But I thought I heard seven or eight shots."

"I had Haney's pistol too."

"I forgot that. Well, your timely gunfire made things a lot easier for me."

"Not all that easy." Felder pointed at

Pike's wound.

"I've had worse."

"What about him?" Felder asked, pointing to Haney, who was sitting up, looking dazed.

"Ain't my concern. He's the town marshal. Town either elected him or had someone appoint him. They can decide what to do with him. Far's I'm concerned, he's almost as bad as these other scum and should be run out of town."

A rumble of assent went through the crowd.

"You likely needn't worry about the other association members, I think. Hungerford's dead. So's Smythe, and Appleyard is wounded. That should discourage any others from trying to do anything else against you all."

"Thanks, Brodie. I . . ."

"Tell Charlie, Viv, and all the others farewell for me."

"You ain't comin' back with me?"

"Reckon not. You people've got enough to do, gettin' back on your feet. They don't need a broke down old saddle bum like me hangin' around." He smiled softly.

"Like hell. Charlie, Viv, and all of 'em will be mighty put out that you just up and left. Especially Marcy." He grinned. "Well, maybe not Marcy after what happened."

"They'll have enough to occupy 'em. They'll have forgotten about me in a month."

"I disagree, but I reckon I can't make you change your mind."

"Nope."

"Well, at least have the doc see to your wounds, get some fresh clothes, and have something to eat. Your horse should have some care, too. I'll keep you company if you like."

Pike thought it over, then nodded. "That sounds good. Long as you don't set there the whole time tryin' to talk me out of leavin'."

"That saddens me, but you got a deal."

ABOUT THE AUTHOR

John Legg has published more than 55 novels, all on Old West themes. *Blood of the Scalphunter* is his latest novel in the field of his main interest — the Rocky Mountain Fur Trade. He first wrote of the fur trade in *Cheyenne Lance,* his initial work.

Cheyenne Lance and *Medicine Wagon* were published while Legg was acquiring a B.A. in Communications and an M.S. in Journalism. Legg has continued his journalism career, and is a copy editor with *The New York Times* News Service.

Since his first two books, Legg has, under his own name, entertained the Western audience with many more tales of man's fight for independence on the Western frontier. In addition, he has had published several historical novels set in the Old West. Among those are *War at Bent's Fort* and *Blood at Fort Bridger.*

In addition, Legg has, under pseudonyms, contributed to the Ramseys, a series that was published by Berkley, and was the sole author of the eight books in the Saddle Tramp series for HarperPaperbacks. He also was the sole author of Wildgun, an eight-book adult Western series from Berkley/Jove. He also has published numerous articles and a nonfiction book — *Shinin' Trails: A Possibles Bag of Fur Trade History* — on the subject.

He is a member of Western Fictioneers.

In addition, he operates JL TextWorks, an editing/critiquing service.